Field Guide to Monsters

Field Guide to Monsters

Darren Zenko

First printed in 2008 10 9 8 7 6 5 4 3 2 1
Printed in Canada

The Publisher: Dragon Hill Publishing Ltd.

Library and Archives Canada Cataloguing in Publication

Zenko, Darren, 1974–
Field guide to monsters / Darren Zenko.

ISBN 978-1-896124-38-4

1. Monsters. I. Title.

GR825.Z45 2009 001.944 C2009-901510-2

Project Director: Gary Whyte
Project Editor: Pat Price
Illustrations: Peter Tyler and Chris "Fish" Griwkowski
Cover Image: Photos.com

We acknowledge the support of the Alberta Foundation for the Arts for our publishing program.

PC: 1

Contents

Chapter 3: Water Monsters

Chapter 4: Animal- and Plant-like Monsters

Preface

What is it that makes some people head out into the lost and the unknown, to step over the edge into the unexplored and unexplained? Why would an author, living a comfortable life with a good and stable future, travel to the four corners of the world—trekking through disease-ridden swamps, damp caves, isolated valleys, bottomless lakes, tangled forests—to confront the monsters that would cause the common man to turn tail and run at the first whiff of danger?

The common man—the man of comfort and leisure—would never dream of leaving it all behind to risk life and limb seeking such dangerous creatures. In his mind, the risk-taker is out there for fame and fortune. Or for the lust of the hunt. Or maybe some primitive, animalistic game of one-upmanship to prove himself better than the next man. But he would be wrong! The true monsterologist thinks not of these petty ends. The thrill of discovery is what he seeks.

And if you were to ask such a man about the danger he faces when approaching the lair of the Werewolf, the cave of the Dragon, the dank swamps of the Mokele-mbembe, how would he respond? There'll be no talk of fear. The experienced crypto-zoologist, with his years of study and deep understanding of each creature's behavior, habits, strengths and weaknesses, has an edge that lets the true adventurer walk away without a scratch. Given the same situation, the ordinary mortal—the smell of fear rank upon him—would meet his doom.

But such explorations *can* be tricky, fraught with hidden dangers! Most of these monsters are too ugly to look upon. And yet others—the Mermaid, the Leprechaun, the Satyr, the Selkie—can draw you in with their beauty or their lies and then turn upon you with no warning.

With *Field Guide to Monsters*, Mr. Zenko has written a special book. His observations, from explorations and studies, will give you a knowledge that until now has been known only to a special few.

With each entry, you are offered a juicy collection of identifying marks, common habitats, eating habits and mating and nesting behaviours.

But most importantly, if you're of a mind to take that steamer up the Amazon to discover the Encantado or trek the hills of Haiti in search of Zombies, Mr. Zenko lays it on the line with knowledge that might well save your life! What's the safest way to approach the creature without making it angry? And how do you resist its powers? Do you move slowly, head down in a state of submission? Or stand tall to show who's boss? And what if the worst should happen and you find yourself facing a suddenly angered monster, ready to chew you up for lunch and pick its teeth with your bones? It's all here. Study it well—you'll be glad you did!

You hold a rare treasure in your hands. This little book is the distillation of years of study by a man dedicated to his calling. Start from page one and read it cover-to-cover, or flip through it until something catches your eye. Either way, this is the closest most of us will dare come to meeting up with these mysterious, fearsome creatures. And we should be thankful for that. As you read about the lives and habits of these otherworldly beasts, you might easily imagine yourself walking alone across the windy moors one dark night, suddenly being chilled to the core by the terrifying scream of the Banshee, warning of impending death.

For now, draw the curtains and pull your chair a little closer to the warmth of the fire—you won't be going anywhere tonight!

Gary Whyte

Publisher

Ghoul

Werewolf

Skeleton

Chapter 1:

Once-human Monsters

It moves with the speed of the wind, driven by a maddening hunger for human flesh, but the most horrible thing about the creature is that it was once a living, warm-blooded human being.

Zombie

Walking dead

They advance slowly, in eerie silence punctuated only by the occasional moan and the sound of feet scraping the ground. From a distance, the horde may appear to be a shambling crowd of normal humans. The truth is revealed on closer inspection: ripped and bloody clothes, gaping wounds, rotting flesh and the nauseating stench of the grave. These are walking corpses, the living dead...*zombies*.

Where do these mindless horrors come from? There's really no easy answer. First and foremost, though, the zombie was once human—and a human body, even (or perhaps especially) a dead one, is a strong and powerful object. Many methods, technological and *magical*, take advantage of this potential to bring about zombification. Even a quick sampling of recorded zombie outbreaks reveals zombies brought to life by evil spells; zombies created by meteorites from space; zombies as the result of secret biochemical experiments; zombies created by strange viruses; zombies as the result of ancient curses; and zombies spawned by radiation from atomic weapons tests. In most cases, zombieism is highly contagious and spread by bites or scratches.

Although zombies can be created in many ways, the method of destroying them is more-or-less universal: go for the head. To function, zombies require a certain portion of the brain tissue to remain intact, and catastrophic damage to the head will stop the creature cold. Single bullets or buried hatchets aren't usually enough, however—your attack must be wholly decapitating. High explosives, firebombs and industrial-strength acid also work well. Extremely low temperatures will not destroy zombies, but they can immobilize them.

Note that, although the word "zombie" is derived from the Haitian voodoo word *zombi*, the true Haitian zombi is *not* undead. It is a living human, turned into a mindless slave by means of powerful drugs—do not blow its head off! Suspected zombie encounters in areas of known voodoo activity call for careful inspection for rotted flesh and other indicators of zombification. Remember the zombie hunter's rule of thumb: "Signs of decay? Fire away!"

Monster Fact

Some types of zombie might want to eat your brain. This is not because they're hungry—being dead, zombies don't need to eat. Those pitiful creatures that crave brains do so because of an unknown chemical imbalance. For them, only brains can ease the pain of being dead.

Ghost

The haunting apparition

Maybe you hear bumps and footfalls in the night or the sound of something being dragged across the floor. Maybe there's a strange cold spot in one corner of the old building housing your company's offices or an eerie "weird feeling" on a certain stairwell in your home. Perhaps you've glimpsed a strange glowing figure late at night or captured an inexplicable *something* on film. It could be that you've seen a dog or cat bristle and growl at nothing. If you have experienced any of these "maybes," then maybe—just maybe—you've encountered a *ghost*.

Research into ghosts is one of the most exciting monsterological fields today, if only because nobody is completely sure about what ghosts really *are*. The classic explanation—that ghosts are manifestations of the spirits of the dead—is still fairly current. But there are countless other theories: for example, ghosts are nonspiritual energy beings; ghosts are psychic projections; ghosts are time-warp effects, just to name a few. There might be some truth to each one of these theories; the range of phenomena called "ghostly," from minor temperature effects and odd noises to full-bodied phantoms that seem able to communicate, is diverse.

We can place ghosts into two broad categories. The first is a repeating apparition, which can be as simple as a cold spot or as complex as a visible specter. These apparitions have no obvious purpose and seldom, if ever, interact with people or the environment. They're less like true monsters and more like a sort of tape loop, playing over and over, and it's often thought that they represent a sort of "psychic imprint" of past events. The second, more frightening, type seems to have some kind of intelligence and often appears to act with purpose. These are the ghosts that write on walls, move objects around and worse. Ghosts of this type can be quite frightening and troublesome, to the point where they behave in a manner similar to the *poltergeist* (p. 196).

Getting rid of a troublesome ghost can be as easy as simply asking the haunt to leave. Try this tactic first should you want to rid your property—or yourself—of an unwanted phantom. An exorcism is, in effect, simply a more forceful way of making this request. Ghosts have been known to follow individuals, and some, especially those of the second type, will not leave until the purpose that binds them to Earth is fulfilled. Determining that purpose can be a long, exhausting and expensive process. Often, a type-two ghost isn't "busted" until a renovation or excavation reveals a body—or body part—in the foundation or walls of a building and the remains are properly buried.

Werewolf

Moon-cursed man-beast

Whether around a camel-dung cook fire or a Coleman camp stove, humans have always huddled closer when they've heard the howling of wolves in the wilderness. It's not the animals themselves that are dangerous—only rarely will wolves attack people—but rather the cunning, bloodthirsty creature that might be running and howling along with the pack under the light of the full moon. The *werewolf*.

Typically, the werewolf is a normal human being afflicted with a transforming curse. This condition is called "lycanthropy," from Lycaeon, an ancient Greek warlord, who was cursed by the gods for the sin of eating human flesh. That's one direct way, among many, of becoming a werewolf. Around the world, there are dozens of curses, rituals and magic spells that are known or rumored to bring on the change. Some werewolf strains can be passed on genetically or even transmitted simply by biting or scratching. Wolves don't have a monopoly on transformation, however: werebears, *werefoxes* (p. 148), weretigers and even wererats are known to exist.

Physically, the werewolf can take three forms: human, wolf and the bestial hybrid form made famous by decades of popular culture. In reality, this third shape is quite uncommon and difficult for the werewolf to maintain. In all forms—even human—the werewolf is phenomenally strong and has the ability to recover almost instantly from wounds. These abilities are tied directly to the phases of the moon, which is the source of the creature's power. On nights of the full moon, the werewolf is an almost-unstoppable killing machine.

The key word, of course, is "almost." Weapons of silver, the precious metal closely associated with the moon, will mortally wound a werewolf, and the herb aconite, also known as monkshood or wolfsbane, will repel the creature—or lethally poison it, if the herb gets into its bloodstream. Certain strains of Eastern European werewolf might also possess a wolf pelt, which they need for their transformation. Destroying the pelt when the creature is in human form will destroy the werewolf as well. The werewolf won't give it up easily, though—best bring along a box of silver bullets and a packet of wolfsbane, just in case.

Skeleton

Mindless minion of bone

They are sounds no explorer of tombs and tunnels ever wants to hear. A clacking and clattering of bone on bone, like a tuneless wooden wind chime; the dragging and clicking of dead, dry, feet on dusty stone; the chattering of grinning, lipless teeth. These are the unmistakable sounds of an approaching animated *skeleton*—the sounds of unthinking, uncaring, unstoppable death.

Animated skeletons are exactly that: bones of the long-dead—usually, but not always, human—brought into an imitation of life by powerful magic. Devoid of muscle or tissue, the skeleton is supported and moved by a field similar to what parapsychologists call *telekinesis*; brainless and mindless, the skeleton moves and fights like a robot, obeying its orders literally. Those orders are given by the *necromancer*—a sorcerer whose powers center on death and the dead—who created it. These evil wizards use animated skeletons as tireless guardians, and, in days past, the skeletons were deployed in battle as fearless shock troops.

But not all animated skeletons are the creations of mad magicians. Some, especially those encountered in tombs, ruins or other ancient holy places, have been animated by a curse or protective spell placed upon the location. When a grave robber, or even a well-meaning explorer, disturbs the protected area, the bones in the tomb—often those of noble warriors buried with their lords for exactly this purpose—rise up to eliminate the intruder. In other cases, the skeletons themselves can be cursed; they are the remains of evil men, whose black souls linger, mindless, to walk their bones about.

Fighting skeletons physically is next to impossible. Although slow and stupid, they can take a lot of punishment before they're rendered harmless. Skeletons can fight headless, armless or legless, and any bone can continue to carry out its murderous instructions. It isn't unusual to see a skeleton's arm dragging itself across the floor by its fingers or even a spinal column thrashing like a snake, trying to wrap itself around its target. Short of smashing a skeleton to dust and bone chips, the only way to stop the bones is to call on another wizard, or a powerful holy man, to dispel the evil enchantment.

Mummy

Instrument of the Pharaohs' vengeance

The burial practices of the afterlife-obsessed people of ancient Egypt are famous for their painstaking complexity. When preparing a royal corpse for burial, its internal organs, with the exception of the heart and kidneys, were removed and embalmed separately from the rest of the body. The brain was removed with a metal hook, via the nostrils, and the skull filled with resin. The body was stuffed with packing and rare herbs and dried using a special salt called natron. It was then carefully wrapped in linen, along with sacred charms and amulets, while prayers were said at every stage of the wrapping. At long last—the process could take as long as two months—the *mummy* was ready to be placed in its final resting place.

For most of Egypt's countless mummies, that was the end of the story—save for those whose rest was disturbed by ancient grave robbers and modern archaeologists, who gave these late pharaohs a new career as museum curiosities. But for certain mummies, those that were perfectly prepared and given the darkest and most secret spells of protection, the story did not end there. The moment the tomb of one of these mummies was violated was the moment they returned to a new and terrible life. The *ka*, or vital spirit, which had been bound for centuries in the burial chamber, returned to its former body, reanimating the mummy as an instrument of vengeance against those who dared to unseal the crypt.

The physical aspect of the mummy is a horror: a shambling corpse, desiccated and leathery, stinking of the grave and draped in the tatters of its linen wrappings, which were ripped apart when the mummy freed its tightly bound arms and legs. It is supernaturally strong, feels no pain and inexorably tracks its victims, to beat or strangle them to death. It is not, however, intelligent; although the ka is the spark of life and the source of base emotion (in this case, rage), it doesn't bear the deceased's intellect. Physically destroying a mummy is, in fact, quite simple: because the thing's body is dry as kindling, it burns quickly and fiercely.

However, if it were truly that easy to destroy, the mummy wouldn't be the feared monster it is. The reanimated corpse is, in reality, more of a symbol—or symptom—of the true nature of the mummy's curse, which is spiritual. Even if the mummy is burned, the curse lingers. Mysterious, incurable diseases, plagues of insects (especially scorpions and scarab beetles), accidents and disasters, nightmares and madness—these are far more dangerous and inescapable than the mummy's strangling hands. It's likely that only the death of the grave robbers will lift the curse and allow the ancient deceased its rest.

Ghoul

Hideous eater of the dead

A battlefield, after the fighting is done, is one of the grimmest, most desolate places imaginable: the earth churned into mud, the still-smoking wreckage of buildings and engines of war, the reek of powder and blood and everywhere the bodies of the fallen. It doesn't take long, once the last shot is fired, for the scavengers to move in—the crows and ravens, buzzards, rats and jackals and the two-legged jackals, the human looters picking the field for valuables. But after these have gone and night has fallen, when the moon shines down on the corpse-strewn pitch, that's when shadowy, shambling figures—hideous *ghouls*—can be seen moving among the carnage, murmuring and groaning in hungry pleasure.

Ghouls are utterly reprehensible creatures, debased scavengers that crave the flesh of the dead. Stooped and stumbling, as pale and bloated as the corpses on which they feed, ghouls are barely intelligent and fear the light of day and the company of the living. Their sunken, fang-filled faces are framed with long, shaggy black hair punctuated with scabby bald spots, and their long, bony fingers end in chipped and yellowed claws. Ghouls, especially female ghouls—known as *ghula*—also have a limited ability to change shape to appear more human. When no corpse meat is readily available, these human-shaped ghouls lure living men and women to feed on them.

Capturing live humans, however, seems to be more of a sport or cruel game for these evil creatures, for they cannot abide the taste of warm, fresh meat. After killing their luckless victim, they will hide the body—or, better yet, bury it in a shallow grave to enhance the flavor—for at least two days before consuming it. A lazy ghoul would much rather have its meals prepared for it, though.

In years past, ghouls digging up fresh graves to feed were a serious problem in cemeteries and churchyards. Modern embalming practices have rendered corpses inedible, however, and ghoul populations in areas using Western-style funeral processes have been nearly wiped out by the reduction in their food supply.

Detecting a ghoul in human form is quite easy; as previously mentioned, the disgusting scavengers are pretty dumb. Their mimicry of human speech is limited to a few parrot-like phrases, making a human-shaped ghoul come across as idiotic. In addition, they're unable to shape-shift away from their horrid odor. Driving off a ghoul is as easy as making loud noises or sudden movements or turning on a bright light; the cowardly things are incredibly skittish.

Monster Fact

Although they appear corpse-like, ghouls are *not* undead. In fact, they are closely related to Arabian *djinn* (p. 80) and still retain some of that species' shape-shifting ability. How such proud and noble creatures became so debased is a mystery perhaps best left unsolved.

Chiang-shih

Hopping vampire of China

On deep and misty nights in China, when the air is filled with dark powers and old omens, you might hear an approaching *thump-thump-thump*, as if a heavy sack was being banged upon the ground. Stay where you are—or worse, get curious and try to find the source of the sound—and you're likely to see a human corpse in the moonlight. Legs and torso swaddled in grave wrappings, arms outstretched, hair white in the moonlight, it hops grotesquely along as it searches blindly for its next meal of human life essence. This creature is one of the *chiang-shih*, China's strange hopping vampires.

The chiang-shih, dead brought back to semi-life by such indignities as death by betrayal, improper burial, grave robbery and evil spells or curses, have more in common with Egyptian mummies than European vampires. A chiang-shih is created when the deceased's higher rational soul departs the body upon death as it should, but, owing to circumstances, the lower, or animal, soul remains behind and takes control of the body. The resulting creature is nearly mindless, too thick even to think of unwrapping its burial linens and driven only by its hunger and hate for the living.

The chiang-shih are capable of drawing out the life essence of their victims by stealing their breath, but, as often as not, the mindless things resort to the classic vampiric method of tearing open their victim's flesh and sucking out the blood. The long, pale hair of some chiang-shih is animate and capable of entangling or whipping victims at long distances, and, like most undead, hopping vampires are nearly impervious to normal weapons, such as guns and spears. They are blind, tracking humans by the smell of their breath and the beating of their hearts.

The chiang-shih can be delayed, but not destroyed, by charms such as red beans, iron filings and garlic cloves. Obstacles knee-height and higher can stop some hopping vampires, but many are known to be capable of superhuman leaps.

Laying a chiang-shih to rest permanently is ideally accomplished by righting the wrong that caused its resurrection, purifying and exorcising the thing's burial plot and driving it back into the grave with a specially blessed straw broom. If the state of the spirit is less of a concern than simply being rid of the monster, it can be dispatched with certain Buddhist and Taoist charms or holy swords. It can also be destroyed simply by burning it with intense flame. Be warned, however: although you can destroy the physical monster by burning, you will still have to deal with the malicious restless spirit.

Wendigo

Cannibal creature of the frozen North

From the woods of Minnesota to the frozen tundra of northern Canada, the nights are often filled with an eerie moaning howl that sets your hair on end and puts ice in the blood of even the most-experienced backwoodsman. In fact, when they hear this cry, wilderness veterans are more frightened than greenhorns, because they know what it is and what it means. That howl is the call of the *wendigo*, and it means doom and death. The creature moves with the speed of the wind, driven by a maddening hunger for human flesh, but the most horrible thing about the creature is that it was once a living, warm-blooded human being.

The wendigo is known by many names throughout its range, among them *witiko*, *windigo* and *windigowak*. Although there have been occasional reports of people being turned into wendigo simply by hearing the cry—it is a literal call of the wild, sweeping victims up and whirling them through the air until their blood freezes and the humanity is harrowed out of them by the wind—the wendigo curse is most often the result of breaking the taboo against cannibalism. The curse is absolute: a snowbound trapper forced by hunger to eat a dead companion is just as likely to be transformed into a bloodthirsty killer. The wendigo-to-be will feel his blood running cold, his heart freezing and his soul filling with a painful craving for human flesh. Transformed into a monster, he will forever walk the wilds and repeat his crime.

The appearance of this literally cold-blooded killer is as varied as its names, a result of its magical nature: the cursed creature takes the shape of local folklore, rather than the other way around. In the southern part of its range, it is generally a monstrous, shaggy, two-legged, snow white beast superficially resembling a yeti.

It stands 15 feet tall, has jagged teeth and ripping claws and gives off a powerful stench of rot and decay. In its northern range, the wendigo is described as a wraith that screeches and moans its way through the woods or as a towering, frost-encrusted skeleton radiating intense cold, in whose enormous ribcage can be seen a polished lump of brilliant blue ice—the heart of the wendigo.

Destruction of a wendigo by melting the heart of ice is no easy task. If the creature has taken physical form, it can be harmed by physical attacks and eventually subdued and restrained. On rare occasions, the cursed victim can be saved by melting the heart gradually in a long and brutal sweat lodge ceremony, but all too often a more direct and permanent remedy—burning the body completely—is called for. If the wendigo is in its ghost-like form, a powerful medicine man must be called on to deal with it through magical means.

Monster Fact

Some wendigo, especially those of the immaterial type, are so powerfully evil that their sickening psychic aura can render an entire village helpless and soul-struck days before the unstoppable creature actually reaches the town.

(This description has been adapted from an account that originally appeared, in substantially different form, in the author's Werewolves and Shape-shifters *[Ghost House, 2004])*

Radioactive Mutant

Grotesque child of the atom

"Fleshy-headed mutant, are you friendly?"

"No way, eh? Radiation has made me an enemy of civilization!"

—from *Strange Brew* (1983)

Throughout the world are places which, through negligence, accident or purposeful action, have been turned into radioactive wastelands—atomic-weapons test ranges, nuclear-waste dump sites and the "exclusion zone" surrounding the ill-fated Chernobyl nuclear reactor in Ukraine. These zones are hostile to human life; they are sources of cancer, respiratory illness and countless other radiation-induced ailments. But even in these wastelands, life, as always, finds a way, and here you'll find grotesque remnants of humanity, those who have been physically, mentally, culturally and genetically twisted by the power of the atom gone wrong—*radioactive mutants*.

Whether they're holdouts of the original inhabitants of the zone, squatters and drifters who arrived later or children born in the zone, all mutants have been changed in some way by radiation. These mutations range from relatively minor alterations, such as scaly skin or misshapen limbs, to major deformations of the human shape: jumbled limbs, multiple eyes, snake-like bodies or body parts that appear to be from another species. It is rumored that mutation can result in superhuman abilities, but if this happens, it's rare. Although mutants are resistant to the lethal effects of radiation, as shown by the fact of their survival, they are not immune; the mutant lifespan rarely exceeds 40 years.

In the isolation and deprivation of their toxic home-steads, mutant culture has generally descended into a degenerate parody of human life. Organization is generally tribal or theocratic—it's common for half-remembered routines of work or play to devolve into mindless religious ritual. Might makes right in their makeshift enclaves, where life is a constant struggle for survival, and malnutrition and infectious disease are as much a danger as the radioactive air and water. Mutants tend to be xenophobic and paranoid, with a jealous hatred of nonmutant humans who happen through their territory—they shoot first and ask questions later. The thought that these sad degenerates might represent the possible future of humanity is chilling.

Vampire

The insidious bloodsucker

Everyone knows the signs. In the moonlight filtering through the fluttering drapes of the open window, a pallid corpse lies drained of blood, with no sign of injury save two deep punctures on the side of the neck—the grisly calling card of the most nefarious of the undead. Time to break out the garlic, crucifixes, holy water and wooden stakes...there's a *vampire* on the prowl.

Vampirism is a type of sorcerous disease, usually transmitted through blood or saliva, that transforms its victims into powerful undead beings who must consume blood to maintain their eternal non-life. At a glance, most vampires appear human, though closer inspection reveals characteristic abnormalities: pale, waxy skin, pronounced canine fangs, cold body temperature. As the centuries of its existence pass, a vampire's appearance becomes more bestial and corpse-like. Eventually, most vampires degenerate into savage creatures known as *nosferatu* (p. 34).

There are hundreds of vampire species, or bloodlines, spread around the world, and their powers vary widely. Common vampiric abilities include superhuman strength, the ability to shape-shift into animal or gaseous form, the ability to mentally command animals (vermin, especially), hypnotism, mind reading, teleportation, bilocation and levitation. Depending on their age, bloodline and geographic origin, an individual bloodsucker can have some or all of these abilities to varying degrees.

Compounding this unpredictability is a corresponding variation in vampiric weaknesses. Although all vampires detest sunlight, for example, some can walk out during the day for short periods, while others disintegrate or burst into flame at the slightest touch of a sunbeam. Some vampire strains can't cross running water, others can't enter private homes unless invited. Many vampires, particularly the major European lines, are repelled by garlic and holy objects, while others could lick spaghetti sauce off a crucifix without harm. Cautious vampire hunters often pack 20 or 30 pounds of gear to cover every contingency; a true veteran does her homework and brings exactly what she needs.

Hunting is one thing, but permanently destroying a vampire is another. Vampires are the most resilient of the undead, able to regenerate and rise again from even a few grams of ash. Utter destruction requires pulling out all the stops: driving a stake through the heart, beheading, exorcism, burning and burial of the ashes at a crossroads.

Frankenstein

The patchwork monster

> "I expected this reception," said the daemon. "All men hate the wretched; how, then, must I be hated, who am miserable beyond all living things! Yet you, my creator, detest and spurn me, thy creature, to whom thou art bound by ties only dissoluble by the annihilation of one of us."
>
> —Mary Shelley, *Frankenstein* (1818)

It's an integral part of human nature to want to exercise that power generally considered to be the exclusive province of a supreme god or creator: the ability to create life. This desire is normally channeled through the arts or the bearing of children, but some men take it to its literal extreme, dabbling with dangerous forces and playing God with their mechanical or magical creations. The most hideous of these are tragic patchwork men, the products of grave robbing and forbidden science. The most famous of these was created by a mad German medical student in 1818, and popular confusion between creator and creation has labeled all these miserable creatures with his name: *Frankenstein*.

A frankenstein is assembled from pieces of exhumed bodies; limbs, organs, torso, head and brain are carefully (or not so carefully, as the case may be) selected and sutured together. This crazy-quilt corpse is then treated with weird chemical solutions so obscure they border on the mystical and readied to receive the spark of life—a surge of electricity that, in Frankenstein's time, could only be derived from a lightning strike. The blast of juice flows through the morbid tissue, and the monster is jolted awake, to begin its strange new life.

Physically, a frankenstein's appearance is dependent on the care and haste of its creator—the secret nature of the work, the means by which bodies are acquired and eagerness to get quick results often produces a rushed and unconsidered selection of parts and sloppy and brutal assembly. The chemical and electrical forces animating the thing give the frankenstein superhuman strength and endurance and resistance to cold and injury. The great weakness of these walking corpses is fire; their chemically treated bodies are especially flammable.

The tragedy of the frankenstein is that, although some have communication difficulties as a result of poor workmanship, they are all thinking, feeling beings. Brought to life by their hubristic creators, they can never enter into human society and are never given an outlet for their intellect and emotions. Despised and bitter, hounded by humanity, these lonely monsters often become dangerously psychotic, even homicidal.

Nosferatu

Bloodsucking parasite in the shadows

A subhuman monster crawling through the shadows, driven by a hunger that is never satisfied; a parasite skulking on the fringes of society, feeding off the life force of humanity; a diseased creature, whose only true companions are the vermin of the underworld—the pathetic and depraved *nosferatu* is the true face of vampirism.

The name "nosferatu" is ancient, the creature popularized in the 20th century by F.W. Murnau's famous 1922 film of the same name. Each nosferatu was once a vampire of the type we're familiar with through Hollywood monster movies, but countless years of cursed non-life and constant hunger for blood eventually take their toll. The skin of the nosferatu is even more pale and unhealthy than it once was, taking on a diseased appearance or greenish tinge, and the teeth and fangs are yellowed, snaggled and even more pronounced. Fingernails harden to claws, the ears either become bat-like or fall off entirely and the face becomes sunken and bestial. After long centuries, there's nothing left of the creature's once-human nature, just a shambling, murderous parody of a man. How long the process takes depends on the individual vampire's personality and willpower, but it will eventually overtake all bloodsuckers that manage to avoid extermination by other means.

As creatures of disease and death, these lesser vampires have a strong bond with rats and other vermin. The power to communicate with and control these animals grows as the nosferatu decays, to the point where a single vampire can be "lord" of an entire city's pest population. As the vampire's intelligence fades, it is replaced by raw animal cunning and great strength—a cornered nosferatu is an incredibly dangerous opponent.

Fortunately, for monster hunters and ordinary citizens, the nosferatu's loss of human willpower gives it greater vulnerability to the usual anti-vampire weapons. Lesser vampires react with great fear and panic to holy symbols, holy water and garlic. Their aversion to light, in particular, becomes so great that even a powerful flashlight can stun a nosferatu. But don't rely on your high beams—a stake through the heart, followed by decapitation and cremation, remains the only way to permanently dispose of the nosferatu.

Monster Fact

The term "nosferatu" comes from the Greek word *nosophoros*, meaning "spreader of disease." In the Middle Ages, it was thought (correctly) that vampires carried the dreaded plague.

Sasquatch

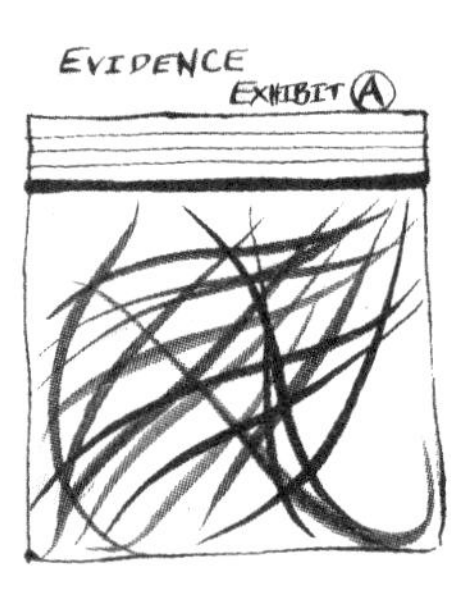

Chapter 2:
More Monster than Human

Although homo sapiens is now the dominant humanoid species on Earth, this was not always the case. Over time, humanoid evolution has wandered down some strange alleys and given us some strange cousins.

Giant

Towering humanoid of legend

Giants hardly need describing; their physical presence is famous and unmistakable. Enormous humanoids ranging in height from 10 to 30 feet and, rarely, even beyond that, they are among the most common of monsters, accompanying humans wherever on Earth we've spread ourselves. Although their size and appearance vary—some are beautiful, many are hideous, and their skin tones range through the rainbow—giants generally have two traits in common: great strength and foul tempers.

The first and greatest of the giant races were the *gigantes*, who are believed to have been born of the Earth when the planet was still very young and from whose name the word "giant" derives. The gigantes were said to be invincible, and some—the so-called *hecatonichres*, or hundred-handed giants—were mutants with multiple limbs and heads and supernatural abilities, such as fire-breathing. According to legend, the gigantes were destroyed and buried after a great battle in prehistoric times, but it is more likely that they simply dispersed and evolved—or devolved—into modern giants and their cousins, such as the *ogres* (p. 46), *trolls* (p. 42) and *cyclopes* (p. 40).

As mentioned, giants can live anywhere humans can, and, through the ages, many of these enormous beings have become legendary. One of the most famous is Goliath of Gath, champion of the Philistines of biblical times; his defeat by the Israelite champion, David, who dispatched the giant with a single sling-stone to the head, became an allegory for the victory of the underdog over overwhelming force. England has its great giants, Albion, Gog and Magog, and Scandinavia has the elemental *jotuns* and the primordial Ymir. North America is also home to giants; stories of the huge woodsman Paul Bunyan are claimed by some to be based on an actual giant whose curiosity about the new settlers and frontiersmen led him to live among them for a time.

Unless you're a modern-day David, physically fighting a giant is pretty hopeless; giants are fond of hurling huge trees and boulders, and they do so with deadly accuracy. However, giants are stereotypically bullies—proud, boastful, not too bright and fundamentally cowardly. If you keep your wits about you, it's likely you'll be able to talk your way out of giant trouble. Aside from certain particular lusts (giants are music fans and cannibals in about equal number), most giants want nothing more than to be left alone...and, for beings so huge, they're certainly good at going undetected.

Cyclops

Massive, one-eyed master blacksmith

Fierce and stubborn, immensely huge and unbelievably strong, master of the arts of metalworking and weapons making, the mighty *cyclops* (plural: *cyclopes*) is easily distinguished from other giants by the single huge eye in the center of its forehead. There are actually two types, or generations, of cyclopes: one that long ago departed our world and another that still works its great forges in the hidden parts of the Earth.

The Elder cyclopes were ancient even before the gods of Olympus were born. For countless millennia, they were imprisoned, first by their father, Uranus, and later by their brother, Cronos, out of fear of their power. When their nephew, Zeus, freed them to get their help overthrowing Cronos, the grateful cyclopes—Argus, Brontes and Steropes—used their skills to forge Zeus' famous thunderbolt weapons. They also crafted the trident of the sea god, Poseidon, the bow of hunting goddess, Artemis, and many other legendary weapons of great power. But, as they say, "live by the sword, die by the sword": when Zeus struck down Apollo's son, Aesclepius, with one of his thunderbolts, the enraged Apollo took his revenge on the weapons' makers, killing them.

The second generation of cyclopes, which still inhabit the Earth today, are said in ancient documents to have sprung up from the blood shed by the dying Uranus. They stand more than 25 feet tall and are astoundingly strong, though not nearly as powerful as their ancient namesakes. They have great abilities as blacksmiths, and, although they are unable to create such godly weapons as Zeus' thunderbolts, cyclopes-forged swords are known to be unbreakable, featherlight and razor-sharp. A chain made by a cyclops is as close to unbreakable as non-magical metal can be, and cyclopean armor protects as well as tank plating.

But, unless you're already well-armed and protected, or have something the cyclops dearly wants, it's not advisable to seek out and commission a piece of work from one of these one-eyed giants. They have little of the grace and cultivation—or intelligence—of the elder generation, and many of them are outright carnivores. A favorite pastime of the easily bored cyclopes is to hurl huge boulders at passing ships and snack on the survivors that wash up on the shores of their volcanic islands. On the plus side, should you end up tangling with a bored and hungry Cyclops, the creature's one weak spot couldn't be more obvious.

Troll

Monstrous thug of Scandinavia

In every corner of the world are large humanoid creatures that split the difference, physically, between true giants and normal humans. Smaller than giants and generally dumber than humans, these brutes live an opportunistic life, dwelling in wilderness areas and avoiding humanity except where and when there's an easy chance for bullying or plunder. The classic example and prototype of these kinds of creatures are the twisted, black-hearted *trolls* of Scandinavia.

Male trolls show their giantish heritage in the wide diversity of physical shapes individuals can take. Their height ranges from 6 to almost 12 feet, and the body is generally powerful and muscular, though scrawny (but still very strong) trolls are not uncommon. Arms, legs, extremities and facial features are twisted and exaggerated from the human model. The leathery sickly green, earth-toned, grey or black skin can be smooth and scaly, knobbed and gnarled or anything in between. The hide is thick and tough as tree bark and rapidly seals up cuts and punctures. Female trolls have never been reliably reported. Descriptions of troll wives vary wildly, if in fact they exist; some Norwegian folklore insists they're stunningly beautiful women of human size.

Although some trolls of higher intelligence make a show of being cultured, and some might have advanced skill in such crafts as metalwork, all trolls are malevolent and aggressive, and most are out-and-out thugs. Sadistic, boastful and petty, trolls are also cowardly and will never willingly pick a fight with anyone they're not sure they can easily beat. Trolls are so vile that they can't even stand each other; they almost always operate alone. Bridges are their favorite places in which to set up extortion ambushes, demanding that travelers pay their "toll." It's easy to trap and intimidate victims on a bridge or knock them over the edge, and the narrow deck means marks who put up a fight can only approach the troll one or two at a time. Plus, a bridge is a cool place under which trolls can hide from the sun.

The sun is a troll's worst enemy—and a troll fighter's best friend. If a troll is caught out in direct sunlight, its hide will quickly begin to bake and harden, until it's as solid as stone. Within minutes of exposure, the troll is completely immobilized and soon dies. If the exposed troll can make it to a dark area in time, the hardened layers can be chipped off. This is quite painful for the troll, but its fast-healing skin allows a quick recovery. Basically big babies, trolls usually run away if someone manages to inflict any kind of pain through their thick hides.

Leprechaun

Gold-hoarding fairy of Ireland

Saucy little green-clad elves skipping cheerfully through Ireland's fields and forests, benign miniature men hoarding shining pots of gold at the end of the rainbow, which they are compelled to fork over if ever a human should catch them. Except for the word "Ireland" and the part about gold hoarding, this popular conception of the *leprechaun* is almost wholly inaccurate. The reality of these small folk is darker, and more dangerous, than this kid-friendly caricature would have you believe.

The cartoon version gets the basic look of the leprechaun mostly right: a little man between two and three feet tall, wearing old-fashioned clothes in earthy colors, predominantly or exclusively green. They almost always wear a hat, and black belts and brass buckles are polished to a high gloss; leprechauns are great show-offs and love to display their fine clothing, a symbol of their hidden wealth. You'll seldom find a leprechaun with a beaming face or apple cheeks, though, unless he's disguised himself to trick or waylay you; the leprechaun is naturally dour and grizzled, with a scheming and distrustful look. Come to think of it, you'll seldom find a leprechaun at all—leprechauns are experts at hiding and evading pursuit.

The leprechauns' famous pots of gold are quite real, however, and, although they're not necessarily cached at the mythical "end of the rainbow," they are as well-hidden as any treasures on Earth. Individual leprechauns hoard their stores over the course of centuries, and they slowly accumulate coins and jewelry that the greedy little creature has tricked out of, extorted or outright robbed from humans over the years. The enchantment of leprechauns is such that if you can capture one and keep your eye on it for a certain length of time, it will be forced to give up the location of its hoard. In practice, doing so is next to impossible, because these fairies are masters of distraction. A favorite leprechaun trick is to pretend to be defeated and present its "captor"—after picking his pockets, of course—with a pot of illusory gold that soon turns into mud, dung or vermin.

Like all fairy folk, leprechauns are powerful creatures and are best avoided at all costs. They are quick to insult and slow to forget, and they delight in robbing, scamming and embarrassing humans. They are generally susceptible to all the usual charms against fairies, such as iron objects and holy symbols, and have the additional weaknesses of money-lust and alcoholism. Watch yourself, though; no trickster likes to be tricked, and, given half a chance, a leprechaun will return any injury with interest.

Ogre

Thug, and then some

Although their individual characters aren't nearly as varied as those of wildly diverse humanity, the world's monstrous humanoids do exhibit a range of personalities. Although uncommon, there *are* gentle and refined *giants* (p. 38), introspective *trolls* (p. 42) and probably even philosophical *blemmyae* (p. 54). The exception to these exceptions is the loathsome race of *ogres*; only in the most rare and strange of cases will you find an ogre that's anything but violent, greedy, stupid and sadistic.

Ogres range in size from the stature of an enormous human to that of a rather short giant: about 7 to 10 feet in height. As tall as they are, they measure at least the same distance in width, providing a stocky, blocky frame for the hundreds of pounds of dense muscle that layer their bodies. Hands and feet are largely out of proportion, and ogreish facial features are grotesque and cartoonish by human standards. It can be difficult to tell males and females apart, either by appearance or behavior, because ogres practice a sort of brutal sexual equality, ogresses being just as loud, aggressive, lusty and mean as their men.

Ogres' universal savagery is hardwired into their brains, which are hair-trigger adrenaline factories; ogres fly into berserk rages at the slightest provocation, and their minds perceive anything and everything as a threat. This savagery goes hand in hand with other adaptations that, monsterologists suggest, helped the ogre species survive through the Ice Age. Their thick, insulating layers of muscle and fat render them all but immune to the elements, and they have an organ, similar to that of dogs, that stores oxygenated red blood for astounding feats of endurance. Finally, and especially, ogres have a bird-like grinding gizzard and cow-like multiple stomachs that, in conjunction with a phenomenal immune system, allow ogres to eat and digest pretty much anything they can cram into their plus-sized mouths.

Monumentally lazy, except in matters of boozing, lust or brawling, ogres never grow crops and greatly prefer petty banditry and the raiding of human trap lines over doing their own hunting. It's true that human flesh is a favorite meal of ogres, but not because of its flavor—ogres barely have a sense of taste. Rather, they enjoy eating humans because a) humans are plentiful, predictable and easy to catch, and b) it's the height of ogre entertainment to torture and kill intelligent beings.

Sasquatch

North America's beloved Bigfoot

In early October 1958, Jerry Crew walked into the offices of the *Humboldt Times*, a small northern California newspaper, with an incredible artifact: a plaster cast of one of several enormous footprints the construction worker found in the mud of Bluff Creek Valley. When his account, complete with the now-famous photo of the giant print, was published on October 5, the shaggy North American "wild man" known as the *sasquatch* gained new fame and a new name: Bigfoot.

The creature's older name was coined in the 1920s by amateur folklorist J.W. Burns, who combined several different but similar Native words, notably the Salish *se'sxac*, to come up with a single name for the wild, hairy giants that appeared in so many stories. It is clear from the tone and style of these legends, which are common to Native peoples from the Yukon south through the Pacific Northwest to north-central California, that the sasquatch is not some mythical or supernatural being but an actual, physical animal. Bigfoot, to the aboriginals of the West Coast, is rare but real.

Both Native folklore and modern evidence give a similar picture of the sasquatch. The creature is a powerful humanoid, from 6 to 10 feet tall, with a broad barrel chest and long arms. The head is sloped and somewhat pointed, with a low forehead, no neck, and a heavily ridged brow. Bigfoot's entire body is covered with short, shaggy hair of uniform length. The hair is dark brown in younger specimens and fades to shades of rust-red with age. The feet are huge, averaging 16 inches long. Although most sightings involve solitary adults, it is assumed that sasquatches form family groups similar to those of other primates—a British Columbian named Albert Ostman reported being held captive by one such family in 1924. Ostman's brief captivity notwithstanding, sasquatches are generally shy and nonaggressive.

The current debate over the sasquatch is not over its existence but its nature. The idea that the Bigfoot is some species of North American ape has been largely abandoned; the body of research has grown to clearly show it as a true hominid, or man-like, creature. Exactly what species it might be—*Gigantopithecus*? *Paranthropus*?—is a matter of conjecture. Until an intact body or live specimen is discovered and examined, the shaggy Wild Man of the Northwest remains a mystery.

Monster Fact

The sasquatch is just one of many similar "wild men" found all over the world. Whether Bigfoot is related to such creatures as the Himalayan yeti, the southeastern "skunk ape" or the Australian Yowie is unknown; research into these elusive humanoids is one of the most active fields in monsterology today.

Golem

Mystical creature of clay

A man-shaped being, created from clay, huge and heavy, its forehead marked with holy words, plodding silently with thudding footsteps as it carries out its creator's orders—this beast is the *golem*, a statue animated by the power of the Kabbalah, the complex and mysterious system of Jewish mysticism. Whether animated for a specific purpose or simply as an exercise in mystical ability, the creation of a golem is one of the most difficult and dangerous feats a Kabbalist can undertake.

The methods for creating a golem vary, and many of the inner details remain hidden from the uninitiated, but all involve a period of intense meditation upon the secrets hidden within the holy letters of the Hebrew alphabet. This meditation is extremely hazardous—one mistake and the would-be golem creator can easily be destroyed by the powers he or she is manipulating. Typically, the golem has a power word—usually *emet*, "truth"—engraved into its forehead. This engraving is the final seal in the animating process, the "on" switch that activates the golem.

The activated golem is a purely robotic creature, like a machine. It has no soul and therefore no will of its own, and it is unable to speak. It receives its orders either verbally or through a magical slip of paper placed under its tongue, and it carries out its instructions to the letter. The quality and refinement of the golem depends on the spiritual perfection of its creator, but, because the power of true creation belongs to God and not to man, all golem are imperfect and must eventually be destroyed or deactivated before they run out of control.

Destroying one of these living statues by direct attack is almost impossible—its heavy clay body resists almost any attack you care to throw at it. The easiest method—easy, that is, if the golem hasn't become violent—is to remove the mystic scroll from under its tongue or to deactivate the power word on its forehead. Removing the letter *aleph* from the word *emet*, for example, leaves the word *met* ("death") and destroys the golem.

Although the secrets of golem creation have largely been lost, a few of the indestructible creatures linger in the world. Strange clay statues should always be approached with appropriate caution.

Monster Fact

One of the most famous golems was created by Rabbi Judah Loew in the late-16th century to protect the persecuted Jews of Prague. Loew's golem eventually had to be deactivated after it became dangerous, but a statue near the entrance of Prague's old Jewish sector commemorates the famous mystical creature.

Sciopod

One-legged vegan of Ethiopia

Filled with descriptions of fantastic creatures, some of which were even accurate, the travelers' tales of the Middle Ages piqued readers' interest with accounts of the strange and monstrous races of men that lived beyond the known reaches of Europe. Giants and dwarves dwelt inthe unknown lands of Asia and Africa, along with one-eyed cyclopes, headless people with faces on their chests, people with ears so huge they served as cloaks and countless races of beast-men. Among these weird deviations from standard-issue humanity were the *Sciopods*, a peaceful race of one-legged men and women.

The Roman scholar Pliny the Elder first described these people in AD 77 in his masterpiece, *Historia Naturalis*, and their name is Latin for "shade foot." Also known as Monoscelans or "monopods," these humanoids were later recreated in stories told by medieval writers such as Thomas de Mandeville, and they regularly appeared in illustrated religious texts, bestiaries and maps of the world. Their native region is often stated as Ethiopia—though they've been reported as far off as Libya—and they're known for their habit of lying on their backs at midday and using a single huge foot as a parasol against the blazing sun. Although the shade keeps them cool, the sun bakes the soles of their feet into hard, black leather.

Having tough soles isn't exactly a drawback, though, because the Sciopods subject their single foot to a lot of punishment as they hop around the countryside. Being one-footed doesn't slow them down, either. The leg is enormously powerful, and the long hops they make can propel them faster than a horse and rider and almost as fast as a gazelle. That strong leg and hardened foot is useful in combat, too; a Sciopod's kick can kill an armored man or break through a brick wall.

Travelers don't have to worry about being chased down and kicked to death by these people, however; unlike some of the more savage humanoids, Sciopods are entirely nonviolent, except as a last resort in self-defense. Not only are they vegetarian, they don't even kill plants. Instead, the Sciopods derive their nourishment from the aroma of the living fruit plants they carry. Should a Sciopod's plant die or be taken from him, the powerful but delicate one-legged creature will soon perish as well.

Monster Fact

As with so many of the so-called "monstrous races," a credible sighting of a Sciopod has not been reported for hundreds of years. Whether they've been pushed back into the wilderness by humans or driven into extinction is unknown. One can only hope that, somewhere in an untouched region of North Africa, these strange but gentle people survive in peace.

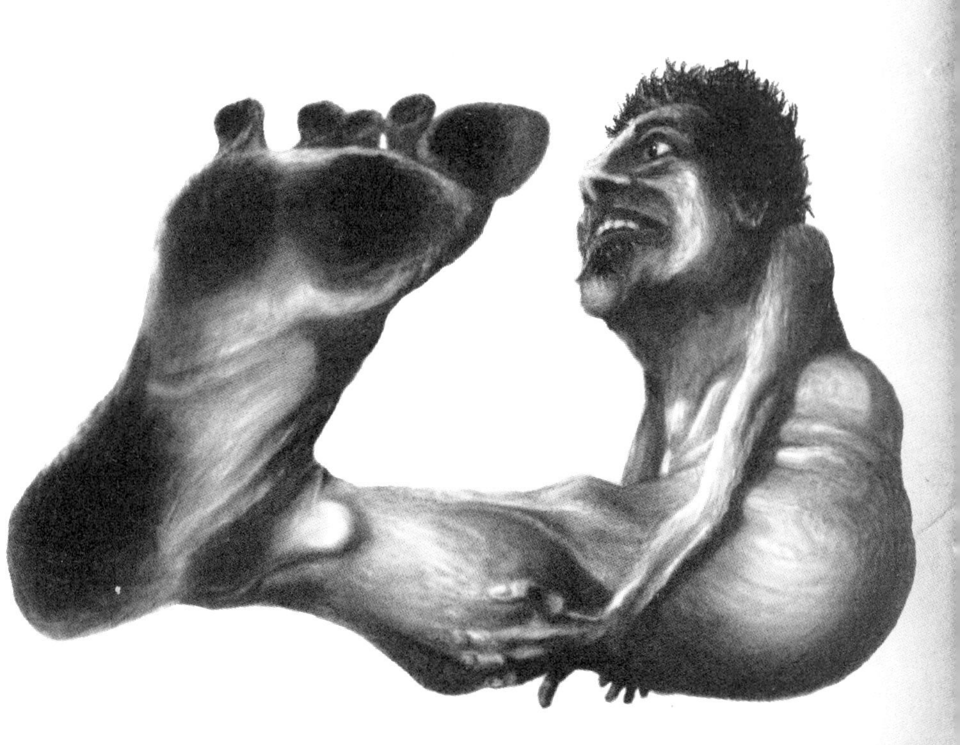

Blemmya

Headless cannibal

From the obscure desert reaches of sun-baked Libya, across northeast Africa, through the mysterious depths of Egypt and the acacia groves of the Sudan, to the highlands of Ethiopia, it is still possible to find, hidden away and fiercely protective of their dwindling little territories, isolated tribes of the strange and savage "Headless Men"—the cannibalistic *blemmyae*.

The blemmyae are enormous humanoids, almost giants, averaging eight feet tall, with powerful shoulders and arms, hands as large as catchers' mitts and legs as thick as tree trunks. Big and tough, their most striking feature is that they have no heads—where a man's neck would begin, a blemmya has only smooth skin over a powerful pair of muscles that give extra strength to its shoulders. The eyes, big as fists, are set in the chest, above a pair of nostrils just below the sternum. The blemmya's mouth—wide and sharp-toothed, muscular but jawless, like a lamprey's—is on the abdomen, allowing it to feed directly into the stomach. Both male and female blemmyae are bearded (though the females lack mustaches), and the beard hangs to the knees, giving the impression of a loincloth.

Socially, the blemmyae are savages through and through. Much less intelligent, on average, than humans—their unimpressive brains, wrapped around the top of the spinal column, must share chest space with the lungs, heart and huge eye sockets—the blemmyae have mastered the arts of fire-making (barely) and club-swinging, and that's about it. Naturally aggressive, fiercely territorial and enthusiastically man-eating, a group of blemmyae can be terrifically dangerous to the unarmed and unprepared. They're not easily frightened off, especially if you've wandered into their territory, and they can't be bribed or bargained with—even if you could speak blemmyae (which is physically impossible for humans); they'd rather just pick your offering from your pockets before slow-roasting you.

As with most humanoids, the Headless Men are on the verge of disappearing; fewer than 1000 blemmyae are thought to survive. Human civilization and the steady expansion of the Sahara desert over the centuries has driven them farther and farther into the depths of the wilderness. In their migrations, the powerful and aggressive blemmyae have driven out many other monstrous tribes before them—pressure from encroaching blemmyae, for example, largely contributed to the extinction of the utterly peaceful and nonviolent, one-legged *Sciopods* (p. 52).

Monster Fact

In his 1582 travelogue, *Divers Voyages Touching the Discovery of America*, geographer Richard Hakluyt describes a blemmyae-like race of headless people, which he called the People of Caora, living in the Americas. Whether this race is a western colony of African blemmyae—and, if so, how they became established in the New World—remains a mystery.

Centaur

The wise and wild horse man

The rugged mountains of Macedonia and northern Greece are the refuge of the tough and intelligent *centaurs*, who once ranged down onto the plains of Thessaly. Centaurs might be the most famous of the world's animal-human hybrid monsters. Almost anybody can tell you what a centaur looks like: the body of a horse with the torso, arms and head of a human. Beyond these basics, however, centaurs can vary in appearance as widely as human races and horse breeds do. These physical variations form the basis of a complex web of tribal divisions, which is one of the main reasons the horse men have never managed to organize themselves into a civilization.

Centaurs are basically wild and resistant to extremes of temperature and weather. They generally do not wear clothing (although they might wear jewelry or tribal symbols), and they do not build structures or form permanent villages. If they need a shelter for a particular reason—such as when Cheiron was raising his young heroes, for example—they make use of natural caves. Although they love to fight with their hooves and fists, they know very well how to make and use weapons, favoring long cavalry lances and their exquisitely crafted short bows.

To say that centaurs are wild and uncivilized is not to say that they are unintelligent. In fact, centaurkind has produced some of the wisest sages in history, especially in the fields of medicine and herbology. It was the centaur Cheiron, for example, who tutored the Greek heroes Jason and Theseus, and so great were his contributions that when he was killed, so the legend goes, the god Zeus placed him in the night sky as the constellation Sagittarius. To this day, people search out centaur wise men in their mountain hideouts, seeking the wisdom they've gained throughout their long lives, which can span three centuries.

But the dual nature expressed in the centaurs´ hybrid bodies extends to their personalities. As wise and learned as a centaur might be, he (or she) is also prone to wild mood swings and impetuous, even foolish, behavior. Centaurs, when they allow themselves to be discovered by visitors, are hospitable, but that hospitality can sometimes turn ugly—centaurs tend to overindulge in food and especially in alcohol, and, when they´re drunk, they have a propensity for brawling and inappropriate lust. The traveler who feasts with centaurs should be prepared to make a quick and discreet exit if things get rowdy—a loaded centaur, who might weigh as much as 2000 pounds, is unpredictable and dangerous.

Scorpion Man

Guardian of the Babylonian wilderness

When he arrived at the mountain range of Mashu,
Which daily keeps watch over sunrise and sunset—
Whose peaks reach to the vault of heaven
Whose breasts reach to the netherworld below—
Scorpion men guard its gate,
Whose terror is awesome and whose glance was death.
Their shimmering halo sweeps the mountains
That at sunrise and sunset keep watch over the sun.
When Gilgamesh beheld them, with fear
And terror darkened his face.
He took hold of his senses and bowed before them.

—from the *Epic of Gilgamesh*, c. 2100 BC

Gilgamesh, the great warrior king of the Mesopotamian city of Uruk almost 5000 years ago, was right to pay respect to the fearsome *scorpion men*. As powerful a fighter as he was, he was also wise enough to know that no mortal—even a demigod such as Gilgamesh—stood a chance against the huge, armor-plated beings that blocked his path to the secret of immortality. An ancient race, personal bodyguards to the great dragon Tiamat before the world as we know it had even been formed, the scorpion men, along with the winged *shedu* (p. 166), were the very symbols of security, steadfastness and righteous defense in the ancient Babylonian world.

The first weapon of the scorpion man is the aura of fear he projects. There's nothing mystical or magical about this—fear is the natural reaction of any intelligent being when challenged by a 12-foot-tall creature with the lower body, legs, armor plates and stinger of an enormous scorpion, the torso and head of a humanoid giant and wicked, saw-toothed pincers for hands. The coloration of their scorpion parts ranges from a relatively bright red-brown to nearly black, and their human skin is a deep tanned olive. Scorpion men are lightning fast in combat, strong enough to smash stone or cut spears in half with their pincers, immune to all poisons and long-lived to the point of being essentially immortal.

As frightening as the scorpion men might be, they are not evil; they just take their guard duty, normally under divine orders, very seriously. In fact, if you're not trying to get past them, they can be friendly and hospitable; in many instances, the places they guard are extremely dangerous, and the morally upright scorpion men have no wish to see humans—even foolish or evil humans—come to harm. Explanation and firm discouragement, rather than violence, are their preferred methods of keeping trespassers and travelers away.

Monster Fact

Although we call them scorpion "men," these beings actually have two sexes. Scorpion women are significantly smaller and less rugged than their male counterparts, but they make up for the difference by being more intelligent and sensitive to the natural and supernatural universe. When Girtablili, the scorpion man who challenged Gilgamesh, wondered aloud what sort of man was approaching, it was his wife who clued him in to the hero's semi-divine nature, saying "his flesh is two parts god and one part human."

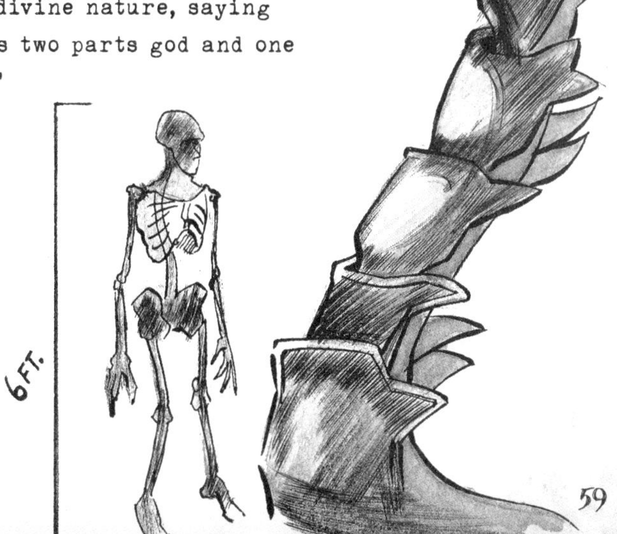

Satyr

Goat-legged party animal

They are the spitting image of the Christian devil: shaggy goat legs ending in cloven hooves, twitching tail of a horse, upper body of a small but powerful human male, buck naked and bronzed red. Curly black hair, long and unwashed, does not conceal the pointed horns extending up and out from the high forehead. Eyes of jade glitter above a wildly grinning mouth full of fangs and laughter, shouting lewd suggestions and singing bawdy songs, encouraging sin and silent only when drinking liquor and eating rich food. A lustful, blasphemous beast-man, a miniature version of Satan made real...a *satyr*.

The problem with this description is that it isn't the satyrs who were made in the image of the devil; it is the devil who was made in theirs. Early Christian missionaries, spreading their message of salvation—and their idea of sin—in pagan territory met stiff resistance from pagan peoples, who worshipped the goat-legged satyrs as gods of nature. The only way to convert these "heathens" was to demonize the satyrs, equating them with the Enemy and eternal damnation. After long centuries of effort, the missionaries were successful. The satyrs—finding humans to be simply *no fun* anymore—withdrew to the depths of the wilderness, and Christianity became the faith of Europe.

Of course, the pagans had it wrong, too. Satyrs aren't gods, though they are religious, devoting themselves entirely to the service and worship of the divine force symbolized by the Greek god of wine and nature, Dionysus. Proper worship of the god meant constant feasting, drinking, singing and all manner of fornication. The fornication aspect poses a puzzle to monsterologists, in that there are apparently no females of the species, yet satyrs are possessed with a sex drive of astounding intensity. Although they constantly seduce or force themselves on human women—as well as nymphs, *dryads* (p. 154), naiads and other female creatures—no infant satyrs are born from these unions. It is not yet known how satyrs reproduce.

An encounter with a group of satyrs (they hate to be alone, unless they're chasing a female) is like an encounter with any group of human drunks—unpredictable, confusing, probably dangerous, possibly enjoyable. Above all, satyrs hate a party pooper, and men who are willing to eat, drink and be merry with them have little to worry about other than a bad hangover—or maybe alcohol poisoning. Women, however, should be warned: satyrs are aggressive and don't take no for an answer. They don't like Mace or pepper spray, either—go for the eyes.

Cynocephalus
The dog-headed man

> Hail O King, I have news for you. I have seen a man with a dog's head on him, and long hair, and eyes glittering like the morning star in his head, and his teeth were like the tusks of a wild boar. I struck him for he was cursing the gods; but he did not strike me, and said it was for the sake of God that he refrained.
>
> —from *The Passion of St. Christopher*
> (tr. Fraser, 1913)

Although homo sapiens is now the dominant humanoid species on Earth, this was not always the case. Over time, humanoid evolution has wandered down some strange alleys and given us some strange cousins—the massive *giants* (p. 38), the headless *blemmyae* (p. 54) and the mysterious *merfolk* (p. 90), to name a few. Most of the "cousins" that survive today do so in isolated pockets in limited geographic areas; they are lost races sliding slowly into extinction. Among the exceptions are the various tribes and clans of the *cynocephali*, the dog-headed men.

Unlike many of the surviving humanoid species, whose range was never great, the cynocephali were and are distributed worldwide, almost as extensively as humans. From the deserts of Egypt, where the jackal-headed Anubis was deified as a god, to the northern ice of Canada, where the shaggy Adlet tribe competed with the human Inuit, the dog men have established themselves. Their cultures and physical appearances are as varied as their homelands. Some are violent and savage, others are peaceful and cultured; some have lean bodies and foxy muzzles, others are stout with pug-like faces. The cynocephali are generally much larger in stature than the average human.

The most famous cynocephalus of all time is certainly the dog man who became known as St. Christopher. Unlike most cynocephali, who have great difficulty speaking human languages, Christopher was blessed with the so-called "gift of tongues" after converting to Christianity. He worked to spread the new faith, performed miracles and was martyred by the savagely anti-Christian Roman emperor, Decius, around the year 250. The body of legend and hyperbole that grew up around St. Christopher became so fantastic and self-contradictory that the Roman Catholic Church eventually proclaimed him to be a mythical figure and "de-sainted" him. He is still venerated in the Orthodox Church.

Modern cynocephali live either in isolated enclaves far from humans or hidden in the shadows of humanity. Going about at night, disguised and hidden, these urban dog men have formed a worldwide network of secret brotherhoods. Theory has it that many *werewolf* (p. 16) reports are, in fact, evidence of cynocephalic activity.

Aigamuxa

Blind running man-eater of South Africa

The diversity of the world's humanoid beings—people with no heads, single legs, animal bodies, multiple limbs, single eyes and on through hundreds of strange combinations—could easily give one the impression that some cosmic idiot child had been given a box of body parts to play with. Usually, however, you'll find some evolutionary rationale, some survival benefit, to even the strangest of variations. But, sometimes, they're just plain weird. Such is the case with the *aigamuxa* of South Africa, whose eyes are on the soles of its feet.

As inconvenient as standing and walking on its eyes might be, the aigamuxa's visual organs—one per foot—are at least well protected; they're surrounded by a ring of cartilage and covered by muscular, leathery eyelids. In all other respects, the aigamuxa are basically humanoid, though covered head to toe with an ape-like pelt of hair. The nostrils are situated high on the round, eyeless skull, with the rest of the face dedicated to a gaping mouth filled with sharp teeth of uniform size. The jaw muscles are exceedingly well developed.

Aigamuxa are extremely fast runners, and they inhabit sand dunes and other areas free of trees or boulders with which they might collide while chasing their prey. Because of their strangely placed eyes, the aigamuxa run blind, having to pause and raise a foot to see the way ahead or keep track of whatever they happen to be hunting; for any kind depth perception, they must lie on their backs and raise both legs. Although they mainly eat antelope and other animals, their favorite meat is human flesh. Aigamuxa are pretechnological and neither use tools nor cook their food, relying on their saw-like teeth as both weapons and food processors.

Though the aigamuxa are exceedingly speedy and possessed of hours' and even days' worth of running endurance, their peculiar physiology makes it easy to get away from them—doubling back or zigzagging while they're running works well. Care must be taken to cover your trail, however; the aigamuxa, when they pause to use their eyes, are excellent trackers. Another option is to scatter broken glass, sharp stones or some type of irritating substance in the aigamuxa's path, in the hope of blinding it. The aigamuxa's tough eyelids, coupled with the fact that they tend to run on the balls of their feet, make this move somewhat iffy.

Rogue Robot

Rampaging metal monster

This world is crawling (and hopping, flying, swimming and teleporting) with monsters; evils lurk in every lake, it seems, and horrors hide in every forest. With so much monstrosity around us, you'd think we wouldn't feel the need to make more. But we do. Throughout history, men and women have been eager to play God, always with tragic results. Some use their knowledge of the biological sciences or the mystical arts; others take pride in the mysteries of human technology, the alchemy of gears and wires and microchips. They create mechanical men, robots, and when even the most benign of these goes bad, the damage caused can be staggering.

The appearance, characteristics and abilities of a robot are unique to each unit—seldom are these technologists' masterpieces mass-produced—and of all monsters, the *rogue robot* is the most physically various. Most are bipedal and built along humanoid lines, but the chassis can be anything from a giant armored hover-tank to a tiny mechanical spider. Some are built for combat and are fitted with strange weapons, but even babysitting androids and artificially intelligent car washers will find lethal ways to use their functions when they go rogue, hugging with bone-crushing force, for example, or polishing a victim's face off.

Given robots' limitless variations in construction and capacity, one might assume that it's impossible to give any general advice on how to deal with them, but most robots share some common weaknesses—don't panic and you'll be okay. First, robots usually have a kill switch or panic button; if it's not obvious, ask the robot's creator where it is—he'll likely be as terrified as everyone else. Next, look for obvious power sources—countless lives might be saved by a simple unplugging or a bucket of paint dumped on a solar panel. Overall, though, the rogue robot's worst weakness will most often be rushed or sloppy construction: exposed wiring and hydraulics, poor waterproofing or a clumsy and inadequate mobility and stabilization system.

Programming for these robots is just as slapdash as their design and assembly, which no doubt contributes to their going berserk in the first place. When a rogue robot can't be stopped by physical means, a psychological approach is called for. Poor logic safeguards mean metaphysical questions such as "What is love?" can cause the robot's program to lock up entirely, and even simple paradoxes, like the old "I always lie/I always tell the truth" trick, are responsible for their share of smoking, sparking robo-brains.

Grey

Mentor or menace?

This book is a guide to monsters "of the world," so the strange beings known as *greys*, whose origins are generally thought to be extraterrestrial, might be technically out of place. But with so many of our supernatural creatures hailing from other planes of existence, it hardly seems fair to exclude such ubiquitous and well-reported beings, simply because they happen to come from outer space.

The greys have become pop-culture icons, so their physical description should be familiar: hairless humanoids of shorter than human stature with disproportionately large heads and bulbous black eyes. The face has only the suggestion of a nose, with two nostrils visible, and the mouth is a toothless, lipless slit. Limbs are long and delicate, with the three-fingered arms reaching to below the knees, and the tone of their cool skin ranges from pale tan to the ashy grey that gives them their name. Greys are seldom seen in clothing, though they occasionally wear equipment harnesses. No external genitalia are visible.

Grey behavior, and the alien reasoning behind it, is more mysterious. They appear to be engaged in some type of research project, the primary fieldwork being the abduction and examination of human subjects. These abductees are taken aboard what is assumed to be the greys' spacecraft and subjected to an array of often baffling, sometimes torturous, probes and procedures before they are released. In most cases, the memory of the experience is wiped from the subject's mind and is only later recalled, if it is recalled at all.

Are the greys benevolent or malicious? Opinions are divided. On the one hand, many abductees and researchers regard the greys with terror, believing them to be an evil or amoral force working against humanity, to the extent of secretly controlling our governments. On the other are those who see the greys as "space brothers," enlightened beings whose mission is to guide humanity into the New Age of peace and perfection. Perhaps the greys´ motives and morality cannot be described in such clear-cut human terms, but one gets the feeling the greys´ true purpose will be revealed sooner, rather than later.

Invunche

Guardian twisted by evil

Monstrous though monsters might be, most have a place, role or niche in either the physical or spiritual ecology of the world. Even the vile, violent, malicious and predatory are supernatural, not *un*natural. The exceptions to these monsters, the unthinkable travesties against nature...*these* are the truly monstrous things that pollute our world. One such is the *invunche* of South America, a twisted parody of life fabricated by pure evil.

The invunche is slave and soldier to the blackest of black magicians, and the method of its creation is a tale of howling inhumanity. It begins with a firstborn boy child, kidnapped by a dark coven of sorcerers or sold or bartered to them by one or both of his parents. One of the child's legs is broken then bent around to his back and fixed there with spells and surgery. From then on, all the slowly transforming child knows is pain, abuse and black magic. As an infant, he is fed the flesh of children; later, he graduates to adult human meat. Strange salves darken and thicken his skin and cause coarse black hairs to sprout over his body. He grows in strength, and his mind is obliterated, until, at last, he reaches adolescence and his transformation to invunche is complete.

The role of the invunche is to guard the sorcerers' secret lair. Fed on goat meat—human sacrifices are too valuable to waste, once the long ritual is completed—it crouches in the dank cave, unable to speak, communicating only in animal grunts and howls. Its weapons are the paralyzing stench of the magical poisons that fill its body and the sheer horror that overcomes intruders at the sight of it. It is strong and tough but clumsy, slow and awkward, hobbling on its two hands and the one crouching foot that can still reach the ground. On the occasions its evil masters need it to travel outside the lair, it is carried by shape-shifting sorcerers with the ability to fly.

But those occasions are rare, for the invunche's place is in the mouth of its masters' lair, the Thing of the Doorstep guarding entry to their Unholy of Unholies. The sight of an invunche isn't a warning, it's a death sentence; the creature isn't the black magicians' first line of defense, it's the last. For the uninitiated, to look upon the form of the invunche, to contemplate the raw horror of the crimes against nature it represents, is to cross a threshold into terminal madness.

Tokoloshe

One-armed, one-legged dwarf of South Africa

We're most vulnerable, physically and psychically, when we're sleeping, so it's no wonder folk traditions the world over are filled with measures to deter the bedroom depredations of the night's creatures. Images of the benevolent *baku* guard the dreams of young Japanese, and western Europeans lay implements of iron at the foot of their beds to ward off witches and malicious fairies. In North America, net-like dream catchers filter out the night's evils, and magic mirrors guard Chinese windowsills. In South Africa, beds are often perched on stacks of bricks, the better to lift their occupants beyond the reach of the night-stalking *tokoloshe*.

These hairy little dwarves are nocturnal creatures, malicious and aggressive, if not outright evil. They are immediately recognizable by their wild shock of hair and single arm and leg. A third member is also uncomfortably conspicuous: the tiny tokoloshe, all of whom are male, possess spectacularly outsized genitalia. Their shortage of limbs and their awkward burden don't slow them down any as they go about their nighttime mischief. Tokoloshe are agile, strong and very tough to catch. Chasing tokoloshe is made even more difficult by their ability to become invisible after swallowing a special magic pebble.

The natural habitat of the tokoloshe are ponds, small lakes, marshes and other small bodies of slow-moving or stagnant water. They come out at night to engage in their two great pastimes: fighting men and having illicit sexual relations with women. In the former, tokoloshe are surprisingly tough, vicious fighters, who come on strong and use every dirty trick in the book. As with many other water imps, such as the Japanese *kappa* (p. 94), the man who gets the better of a tokoloshe might be rewarded with a portion of the creature's magical knowledge. Women seduced or assaulted by tokoloshe might, rarely, bear a child from the union. These halfling children often grow up to become powerful magicians.

Tokoloshe are, in general, fairly easy to ward off with simple charms and precautions and, unlike many small folk, aren't particularly inclined to plague any household in particular. The exception is when a tokoloshe has been commanded (or bribed) by a malicious witch or sorcerer to afflict a specific person or family. In these cases, the tokoloshe is very difficult to exorcise, and a witch doctor or shaman must be called in to break the infestation and track down the magician who ordered the dwarf to its nasty work.

Flying Heads

Airborne horrors of North America

Although the encroachment and expansion of modern society has exterminated whole species and pushed others into hiding in the few remaining wild places, North America once had a fantastic monstrous diversity. The *wendigo* (p. 26) stalked the northern forests, *thunderbirds* (p. 186) and *piasa* (p. 172,) soared through the air and countless weird *giants* (p. 38) stomped across the land. Of these creatures, many of which survive only in sacred Native lore, few are as bizarre as the notorious *flying heads*.

These monsters are, as their name suggests, grotesque and bodiless human or semi-human heads that are capable of flying. Size ranges from that of a normal head to upwards of eight feet in diameter, and the whole head is surrounded by a wild and matted mane of black hair and beard. The mouth is broad and gaping, lined with multiple rows of sharp teeth, and from the temples sprout a pair of great, black bird's wings. One theory on the origin of the flying heads suggests that they are the surviving remains of giants or sorcerers (or sorceresses) of great power that have been decapitated. Many flying heads appear to have a stump of a neck that drips toxic or acidic blood, which would seem to bear this theory out.

Although some flying heads might at one time have had some kind of revenge motive, most are now motivated by one thing only: hunger. Voracious carnivores, they devour any and all living creatures they encounter and are especially fond of human flesh. They hunt at night, screeching and laughing hysterically as they fly through the dark at great speed in search of prey. During the day, they sleep or lie dormant in hidden caves—although a group of smaller flying heads might make their nest in the remains of a village they have wiped out. These desolate ruins are places of great evil power, tainting the countryside for miles around and attracting other unwholesome species.

Perhaps ironically for creatures that are all head, their great weakness is their exceptional stupidity. They are of nearly animal-level intelligence, driven only by their desire to eat, but retain just enough brain power to fall for all kinds of simple tricks and deceptions. Although aggressive and dangerous, they are also quite cowardly. As supernatural creatures of evil, they are also vulnerable to a variety of medicine charms and have a particular aversion to sacred songs and dances.

Harpy

Murderous bird woman

They come screeching and screaming out of the skies, diving out of the blinding sun like hunting hawks, their enormous wings casting predator shadows on their terrified human prey. Snatching up their victims in their huge talons, the nightmare creatures rend them in the air or dash them to the rocks below, where they can dine at their leisure. The whole ordeal might take only a few seconds, but, where *harpies* fly, gruesome death follows.

Originally a Mediterranean species, the harpy's range has expanded since ancient times to follow global shipping routes throughout the tropics and subtropics; sea cliffs and rocky islands are their preferred dwellings and sailors their favorite prey. The harpy has a vulture-like body, taloned feet and the torso and head of a hideous old woman whose fingers end in steel-hard claws. Its wingspan can extend to 20 feet, and the ratty and unhealthy-looking plumage reeks of the foul stench of decaying flesh.

Despite their human features, harpies have no real intelligence, only animal cunning and bloodthirsty instincts. They hunt as birds of prey, diving down onto their preferred victims as they stand exposed on their ship decks. Even when harpies have killed enough to feed themselves, they often continue their assault out of sheer murderous pleasure, leaving the corpses they don't immediately consume on the rocks for a few days—a partially rotted victim is a harpy delicacy.

When attacking, harpies are lightning-fast and relentless, relying on speed, surprise and violence to create bloody havoc before their victims can mount a defense.

Worse, harpies are known to be commanded by the fearsome *erinyes* (p. 170) as assassins, shock troops and kidnappers; better to be torn to bits by the mindless harpies than to be borne away to the lairs of their dark masters.

Tengu

Bird man of the Japanese mountains

The teeming overcrowding that is a defining characteristic of Japan in the popular imagination isn't simply a result of too many people in a small country. It's the result of too many people in a small country with an almost negligible percentage of flat land suitable for cultivation or urban development. The interior of the country is a wilderness of volcanic peaks and sheer-sided valleys, and so almost all of Japan's millions are crowded into the coastal lowlands. Throughout the centuries, these mountain crags and gorges have provided a secure refuge not only for human fugitives, such as the Heike clan, which fled to the remote Iya valley on Shikoku island in the 12th century after their defeat at the hands of the rival Taira clan, but for Japan's ancient race of bird men, the noble *tengu*.

Tengu exhibit remarkable physical variations; they range in height from five to eight feet (size seems to depend on age and status) and in color from the common fire-engine red to warm gold and a rare iridescent olive. They have largely human features, aside from their large beaks, which have often (erroneously) been depicted in art as long, bulbous noses. Their bodies resemble those of a barrel-chested man—the exceptions being taloned feet, a light coat of fine feathers in place of human body hair, and a pair of majestic feathered wings sprouting from the back. These wings enable them to fly quite well, though, like most humans, they prefer not to work any harder than they have to and glide on air currents whenever they can.

Tengu are organized into independent clans that can quarrel with each other but rarely go to war, their numbers in modern times being too few to waste on blood feuds. Their society is learned and technological, and, like many of the world's beast-men—the *centaurs* (p. 56) of Greece, for example—they know many secrets that humans have lost or forgotten. The expertise of the tengu is the science of sword fighting. Even the clumsiest tengu is, by human standards, a master of swordplay, and they are often sought out by warriors eager to learn their secrets. In most cases, the tengu refuse to teach, accepting only the greatest of human heroes into their fencing schools. No human could possibly speak or understand their complex language, so the tengu teach through their modest telepathic abilities.

Although the tengu are wise and civilized, they are generally not much smarter, on average, than humans. Japan's history is packed with stories of human pranksters putting one over on a tengu, tricking the bird man out of some secret lore or magical item. Unfortunately, the proud tengu simply can't take a joke, and, when they take their revenge—and they *will* take their revenge—it's usually quite unpleasant for the smarty-pants human. How unpleasant depends on the circumstances and the bird man's temperament; like the samurai, the tengu see nothing wrong with killing to avenge an insult.

Djinn

Elemental spirit of the desert

In the scorching winds of the Sahara, the scouring sandstorms of the Arabian desert, the gusts that howl through Egyptian valleys; in the whirlwinds, waterspouts and the burning, bone-dry breezes that blow across the North African wastelands—here is where you'll find the *djinn*, wild elemental spirits of air and fire.

Djinn are among the most powerful and intelligent of spirit creatures; in addition to their ability to fly tirelessly at great speeds over long distances and to their command over wind and storms, many djinn have learned great magical secrets over their millennia-long lives. Although they are invisible and immaterial in their natural state, djinn are able to take on solid form—usually that of a giant humanoid warrior or terrible monster—and in this state canpossess immense physical strength. Djinn, tricksters at heart, are also known to take the form of beautiful maidens, though true female djinn—*djinnyeh*—are quite rare, accounting for perhaps 10 percent of the population.

The "genie" of pop culture—the whole bit with the lamp and the three wishes or the sitcom servant in the belly-dancer outfit—is a simplification and distortion of the djinn. First, though skilled wizards and certain holy men can summon and command djinn for their own purposes, it is beyond unlikely that such a mighty and unpredictable servant would be bound in such a way that anyone picking up its vessel could simply give it a rub and access the djinn. Second, a djinn doesn't simply "grant wishes." A djinn has a lot of power, and it will do everything in its power to obey a command if it must, but it can't simply nod its head and cause, say, a house-sized pile of gold bars to pop into existence.

Commanding a djinn is a terrifically dangerous business. These elemental creatures of the wind prize their freedom highly, and they resent being imprisoned or bossed around. They will obey orders in the most literal fashion, always looking for a way to turn them back on the commander, with results ranging from discomfort to catastrophe, depending on the djinn's temperament. Those sorcerers and summoners who make a habit of dealing with djinn are more lawyer than wizard, drawing up elaborate loophole-proof contracts that can run dozens of pages for even the simplest of commands.

Sea Serpent

Ahuitzotl

Chapter 3:
Water Monsters

Beneath its hundreds of millions of square miles of waves, the black reaches of the sea hold secrets we've only begun to realize. Here lie the darker, older things told of in ancient mariners' tales.

Ahuitzotl

The Aztec water opossum

Every corner of the globe has its share—and sometimes more than its share—of "reach-out-and-grab-you" monsters that lurk beneath the surface of its lakes, rivers and seas. It's an important monsterological niche, and it's filled by a dazzling variety of creatures, from the reptilian humanoid *kappa* (p. 94) of Japan to the "water cougar," *mishipizhiw* (p. 108), of North America. One of the strangest of these was known to the ancient Aztecs of Mexico as *ahuitzotl*, the water opossum.

The ahuitzotl's body has more in common with a dog than an opossum, although any canine comparison ends at the legs and feet. The ahuitzotl's legs bend more like an alligator's than a dog's, and the feet are wide and webbed for swimming, the front paws having monkey-like fingers. Its face is dog-like but without ears, and the nostrils are on top of the snout, allowing the ahuitzotl to breathe while just below the water's surface. The only opossum-like thing about the creature is its long, muscular, prehensile tail, which is tipped with a three-fingered, two-thumbed hand.

The ahuitzotl's diet consists of human flesh, which it obtains in classic water monster fashion—sneaking up submerged and unseen, reaching up into a boat with its tail, clapping its hand over its victim's mouth to muffle his screams and dragging its dinner down. The ahuitzotl is a very picky eater and generally consumes only the eyes, teeth and fingernails of its victims. When the corpse of a supposedly drowned Aztec fisherman was found with these delicacies removed, all knew the water opossum was at large, and a priest would be called to perform special funeral rites.

The ahuitzotl is now thought to be extinct, or largely so. Its key habitat, the canals and wetlands surrounding the golden Aztec lake-city of Tenochtitlán, was filled in long ago and now lies beneath the sprawling concrete maze of modern-day Mexico City.

Monster Fact

The eighth Aztec emperor was named for this water beast. The Aztec empire was at its peak under Ahuitzotl's rule, which was legendarily violent: after rebuilding the Great Temple, Emperor Ahuitzotl sanctified it with the blood of more than 50,000 sacrifices. Scores of priests, working in shifts, labored nonstop for days to kill them all.

Encantado

Dolphin man of the Amazon River

It's festival time on the Amazon River, and the handsome young stranger in the spotless white linen suit glides through the noise and music of the party with liquid grace. The girls can't take their eyes off him, but he seems to have eyes for only one. They dance the night away—he's a remarkable dancer—and, sometime shortly before midnight, they slip away from the festivities for a walk along the river. Neither the girl nor the mysterious young man is ever seen again. The next morning, a pair of shoes and a discarded party dress will be found on the riverbank. The old folks will turn to each other and whisper a single name: "*encantado*."

The encantado—Portuguese for "enchanted ones"—are river-dwelling spirits that can take human (usually male) form or the form of a *boto*, the bizarre, long-beaked freshwater dolphins that live in the Amazon. In human form, they are pale-skinned and graceful, usually dressed in bright white clothes of an old-fashioned style. Their transformation is never fully complete, however: an encantado always has a bald spot on top of its head where its dolphin blowhole remains. For this reason, the encantado will usually wear a broad-brimmed straw hat or even a toupee. The encantado is usually more successful at assuming its dolphin form, although boto with flippers ending in human hands have been reported.

The encantado are curious about human society and are particularly fond of festivals and parties, where they can enjoy music and dancing. It is not unheard of for an enchanted one to dwell on land long-term, making a living as a musician. However, this fascination with people shows its dark side when a love-struck encantado tries to take a human girl back to its home in the underwater city called the Encante. Most of these girls never return from this mystic place, and those who somehow escape their dolphin abductors are never quite the same. Many return pregnant, and this happens often enough that it's common in some areas for any child whose father is unknown to be called a "child of the boto."

These water spirits have great powers of hypnosis and suggestion, and they often place their victims under their spell before taking them away. In these cases, it is critical to keep the victim away from the river, using restraints, if necessary, for she will be drawn to the water, pulled irresistibly by the power of the encantado. To break the spell, a medicine man or wise woman must cast a magical powder—manioc flour and crushed dried chili peppers work well—over the water in which the encantado is known to appear. This powder usually breaks the spell and drives the creature away, and any gifts it has given the victim, such as jewelry and fine clothes, will revert to their true forms: rotting leaves and other river trash.

Selkie

Shape-shifting seal woman

Along the coastlines of the British Isles, in the tough little towns that make their living from the sea, it's rare to find a pub or inn where, after a pint or two to loosen tongues, a traveler won't find someone to tell the tale: an old fisherman, living alone—perhaps he's a widower—suddenly finding himself a pretty young wife. A stranger to the area, there's something otherworldly about her, a sadness, a loneliness that sets her apart and keeps her apart. Perhaps she bears him children, perhaps not, but one day—it might take months, it might take years—she's gone as abruptly as she arrived. The deserted man, heartbroken and embittered, dogged by disaster and bad luck, refuses to speak of her. But the people of the village know who and what it was he'd brought into his household: a seal woman, a *selkie*.

In the sea, where they're happiest and most comfortable, selkies take the form of seal cows and live among those marine animals, but their dual nature compels them to leave the water occasionally. Stripping off and hiding her magic sealskin, a selkie takes the form of a lovely young woman, to bask in the sun and salt spray, brush her long hair and enjoy her human voice while singing sweetly to herself. This is the time when she is most vulnerable. Any man finding her cached sealskin literally holds her life in his hands—without it, she cannot transform; if it's destroyed, she dies. In this way, the wild and beautiful selkie is extorted into a landlocked marriage.

Long-term life on land is, for the amphibious selkie, an almost unbearable bondage. No matter how loving or doting her husband/captor might be, she pines constantly for the sea. Preventing her return to the water is a terrible crime against her dual nature. But nature, even magical nature, has a way of winning out in the end, though it might take decades. Whether by chance, or with the assistance of her half-human offspring, the selkie will contrive to regain her sealskin and, taking her children with her, will return to the sea.

From that moment until his death (usually by drowning), the unfortunate man who has captured and lost a seal wife is the enemy of all the people of the sea. His nets tangle and tear, storms and fog seem to follow him, and other sailors and fishermen, wary of his obvious bad luck, avoid his boat like it was a plague ship. But, as is usual when dealing with creatures of magic, the reverse is also true—anyone performing a kindness toward a selkie will have little to fear from misfortunes at sea.

Monster Fact

Beings strikingly similar to the selkie are known in almost every corner of the world, from the sea dragon maidens of Japan to the goose women known to the Inuit of the Arctic. A removable animal hide is common to several land-based shape-shifters, as well, leading some researchers to identify the selkie and her cousins as a class of were-creature.

Merfolk

People of the sea

Whether romanticized as the tragic heroines of magical love stories, stigmatized as omens of shipwreck and disaster, feared as temptresses luring men to their deaths, or—most insulting of all—dismissed as imaginative sailors' accounts of seals or manatees, few creatures have been as idealized and misrepresented as the mermaid. In reality, sea women are members of one of the most diverse and vibrant peoples with whom we share the planet—the *merfolk*.

The people of the sea hardly need describing here, as the popular conception is generally accurate: beings with upper bodies similar to those of terrestrial humans and lower bodies resembling the body of a fish. Details of coloration and physiology vary from region to region, but all mermaids and mermen are warm-blooded, mammalian, water-breathing and thoroughly suited to life in the sea. A very few merfolk—perhaps one in 1000 females and one in 10,000 males—have the natural ability to assume terrestrial human form. Merfolk magical science is generally highly advanced and specialized in transformation magic, so shape-shifting charms are relatively easy to come by for individuals who wish to mingle with air breathers.

The world's merfolk are divided into nations, and their various cultures are as different from each other as those of humans. There are kingdoms and dictatorships under the sea, as well as democracies and communal groups. Some merfolk nations are civilized, while others are primitive tribes. One corner of the ocean might be home to peaceful kelp farmers and fish ranchers, another can be the domain of fierce warriors, who charge into battle armed with nets and tridents, protected by armor of shell and coral and pulled by their *hippocampi* (p. 102) warhorses. All merfolk nations are preindustrial, though metals and artifacts scavenged from human shipwrecks are commonly used.

Merfolk attitudes toward surface dwellers range from concerned curiosity to outright hatred; human shipping, overfishing, whaling and pollution have had a profoundly negative impact on the sea people's economy and ecology. Merfolk nations that once lived on the bountiful coastal shelves have been driven into deeper waters by human encroachment. Any merfolk encountered within a few miles of an urban coastline are likely to be raiders on missions of sabotage and metal gathering and will have a "stab first, ask questions later" approach to any and all air breathers.

Rusalka

Drowned soul stealer

Murder and betrayal, sudden death or death with unfinished business, tragedy or pre-death trauma: a variety of factors can cause a human spirit to remain bound to the Earth, when it would have otherwise have passed on. Commonly, this means persistence as a *ghost* (p. 14), but there are worse fates. Consider the sad *rusalka* of Russia, drowned girls whose spirits are doomed forever to endure in the water as soul-stealing creatures of nightmare.

In appearance, the rusalka is an idealized projection of the girl she was in life or perhaps the woman she would have become. She has flawless skin that shines with a silver glow in the moonlight, long hair that swirls about her, as though it floated in the water, and a lithe, young body that is perfect and enticing. She sings in the night with a voice like delicate flutes and chimes and dances with the grace of waves lapping the shore. Irresistible, she lures men, women and children to join her in death by drowning.

But it is the children in whom the rusalka is particularly interested. In the mindless torment of her hellish afterlife, the rusalka's beauty becomes her single-minded obsession, and it is the energy from children's souls that maintains her eternal perfection. Only the unbaptised will do—baptism puts a child's soul beyond her reach—so the rusalka is drawn by the sound of a woman in labor or the cries of a newborn baby. Some deranged rusalka, long lost in their doom, will even go so far as to use their power to suck the soul out of an unborn child, resulting in stillbirth. The rusalka consumes the soul energy directly; tales of rusalka boiling children in cauldrons to offer them up to the devil are the result of confusion with the anti-pagan scare stories of Christian missionaries.

As you might imagine, the rusalka is of great concern to the women of the Russian countryside, and many effective measures have been taken to protect against them. Foremost is the offering of womanly things—fine linens, embroidered kerchiefs and other household fabrics—to the rusalka, not simply as gifts but to remind the spirit of its former humanity. Holy symbols, especially the crucifix, are also effective. Finally, many rusalka were themselves victims of the *vodianoi* (p. 96) and were lured to their deaths by that evil spirit to serve as wives. Exorcising or driving away the controlling vodianoi can free the rusalka from her bondage to the water.

Kappa

Polite amphibian bloodsucker

When the heat and humidity of summer comes to the Japanese countryside, it's not unusual to see people, most often the wiser members of the older generation, tossing fresh cucumbers into the rivers and canals that flow near their homes. Look closely at these vegetables and you might be able to read the names and ages of family members carved into their glossy green surfaces. The offerings are tossed into the water at the start of swimming season in the hope of saving loved ones from the clutches of the dreaded *kappa*—the crisp veggies are the only thing the creatures crave more than human blood.

The amphibious kappa inhabit waterways and lakes all over Japan, lurking beneath the surface in wait for careless swimmers or people strolling alone beside rural canals. Pop-eyed, slimy-skinned and protected by a tortoise-like shell on its back, the kappa's strangest feature is the shallow reservoir on the top of its head in which it stores the water it needs to survive on dry land. Kappa are amazingly strong, despite their childlike size. Once they get a victim into the water, escape is nearly impossible, and the kappa will greedily draw out the vital fluids through any available orifice.

Although bloodthirsty, kappa are highly intelligent and know many deep secrets of medicine and healing. They don't readily share these secrets with humans, of course, but a human who somehow gains the upper hand against a kappa might be able to force the slippery little creature to give up a bit of its hidden wisdom. There are reports of survivors of kappa encounters coming away with remarkable skills at setting bones and curing illness.

But how do you survive an encounter? First, keep your cool: you probably won't be able to outrun or outfight a kappa, and you *certainly* won't be able to outswim it. Second, remember your manners. A kappa is a refined and cultured creature; if you bow politely, it could never be so rude as to not return the gesture. Bending forward, it will spill its precious reservoir of water and lose its strength and power. Helpless, it will be at your mercy.

And mercy is exactly what you should show: as with "little folk" all over the world, mistreatment of one kappa can earn you a lifetime of grief from all its people.

Vodianoi

Russian water demon

As with all of Earth's wild places, the plains, forests, hills and rivers of Russia's vast expanses are home to spirits of countless variety. Some, such as the household spirits known as *domovoi*, are generally benevolent, causing mischief only when annoyed by human laziness or impiety. Others, such as the *leshiye*, or forest goblin (p. 152), are more sinister and threatening to people. But none is more malignant, more dangerous, more in touch with what the Russians call *nechistaia sila*—"the unclean force"—than the watery *vodianoi*.

Like most nature spirits, the vodianoi is a powerful shape-shifter, able to take on any form it chooses to deceive its victims. Its most common appearance, however, is that of a grotesque old man. In this shape, the vodianoi has a long and weedy beard dripping with foul water, blotchy and blemished green skin mottled with mosses and pond scum, ugly snaggled teeth and a slimy lower body like that of a diseased fish. It dwells mainly in the mucky shallows of lakes, stagnant ponds or fouled and sluggish streams, where it waits for the unwise and unwary.

Drowning people is the vodianoi's pride and pleasure. Sometimes, the evil creature takes the direct route—simply grabbing lone passersby and dragging them down—but more often it enjoys a drawn-out process of deception. The vodianoi can even seem to be actively helpful, but, unless its chosen victim is especially clever or resourceful, the vodianoi's final gifts will be two lungfuls of foul water. It is through drowning that the vodianoi sometimes take their wives, or *vodianikha*. Luring and drowning a young woman, the vodianoi binds her spirit to the water as a *rusalka* (p. 92), in whose form the unfortunate girl will be doomed to dwell—and kill—along with her twisted "husband."

Evil as they are, the vodianoi, like all spirits, are bound by magical rules that even they must obey. Certain offerings—especially Russia's "big three": bread, salt and vodka—presented with due respect will placate the vodianoi, and rare black roosters are known to be a powerful talisman against the demonic water spirits. Exorcism of the body of water in which a vodianoi is known to reside can be an effective and permanent way to drive the thing away, but the process, as always, is very dangerous to all involved. One wrong word or gesture, and the vodianoi will have its revenge.

Lake Monsters

There's something in the water...

In the year 565, near the cold shores of Scotland's deep, dark Loch Ness, a huge, snake-like head and neck broke the surface of the black water and loomed over a lone salmon fisherman. There were many legends of evil water monsters living in the loch, and the terrified man screamed for help, dove into the frigid water and began thrashing his way back to shore as the strange creature pursued him. The Christian missionary St. Columba heard the man's cries and, ordering the thing back in the name of God, succeeded in driving it away. By the time innkeeper John Mackay reported the first modern sighting of the *Loch Ness Monster* 14 centuries later, the creature had mellowed somewhat and was eluding humans, rather than chasing them. Hundreds of sightings have followed Mackay's report, making "Nessie" the world's most famous *lake monster*—and perhaps the most famous monster, period.

But the creature in Loch Ness is only one of perhaps hundreds of mysterious things that lurk in the depths of lakes around the world. Two of the best known specimens are North American. A beast known as "*Champ*" inhabits Lake Champlain in upstate New York, and a photo taken in 1977 by Sandra Mansi, though blurry and poorly exposed, remains one of the best images we have of this remarkably elusive monster. Lake Okanagan in British Columbia, meanwhile, is home to *Ogopogo*, which has been reliably reported scores of times, beginning with the very earliest European expeditions to the area.

No living specimen, recognizable corpse or detailed photograph of a lake monster has ever come to light, and there is considerable debate over their nature. There might be several entirely different species inhabiting the world's lakes: Nessie and Champ, for example, are generally described in a form similar to the plesiosaur, an aquatic dinosaur assumed to be long extinct. Ogopogo is consistently serpentine, with the humps or coils of its long body breaking the water's surface. Most researchers assume a reptilian nature for lake monsters, but there is speculation that at least some of the creatures might represent an unknown type of freshwater seal.

Hunting lake monsters is one of the most active and well-funded areas of monsterological research today. Sometimes dozens of teams work simultaneously around the world, using divers, sonar, lasers, underwater cameras and microphones—and even magicians and psychics—in a race to be the first to bring Nessie and its fellows into the light of science. So far, it would seem that the lake monsters prefer the darkness of the deep, cold lakes they call home.

Monster Fact

Lake monsters like their lakes big, deep and cold. Lake Okanagan is almost 80 miles long and 800 feet deep, and Lake Champlain stretches more than 100 miles and drops to 400 feet deep. And though Loch Ness, the largest lake in the British Isles, is "only" 24 miles long, its deepest point lies more than 900 feet beneath the surface!

Kaiju

Giant monster of the Pacific

It's one of the most awesome, terrible scenes imaginable: the surface of the Pacific, surging as though before an approaching tidal wave, cresting and churning a half a mile, or so, from the shore; a huge dark shape emerges from the roiling surf, streaming white water. Glowing eyes break the surface, then an enormous jaw filled with gleaming teeth, then the impossible bulk of a reptilian body taller than a 10-story building. Air-raid sirens wail as the massive thing lets out an ear-piercing scream of rage and challenge—a *kaiju* is coming ashore, and nothing can stand in its path.

Kaiju is Japanese for "giant monster." It is a general term for any of the various creatures, ranging from 50 to 150 feet tall that are known to inhabit a large area of the Pacific (on land as well as in the sea) centered around the Sea of Japan. Although several ancient records of giant creatures exist in the region, only since the middle of the 20th century have kaiju been appearing in great numbers. Researchers speculate that factors such as nuclear tests, deep-sea oil drilling and industrial pollution have disturbed long-dormant monsters—or that radiation and pollution have somehow *created* the kaiju through mutation. Kaiju are generally reptilian in nature, although avian, insectoid and mammalian specimens are known. Whether a 60-foot ape reported in Africa should be classed with the kaiju is a matter of ongoing debate.

Kaiju are drawn to cities and human industrial activity, and a single giant monster can cause thousands of deaths and billions of dollars in property damage as it smashes its way across the landscape. Making matters worse is the tendency for kaiju to fight each other—the appearance of one giant monster almost guarantees the arrival of a challenger. These combats sometimes escalate into multimonster *battles royale*, in which the devastation is nothing short of apocalyptic. Most kaiju can breathe fire, emit energy beams or deploy some other exotic attack. Exactly *why* the kaiju fight is unknown. Some researchers call it basic territorial instinct; others have noted signs of intelligence, alliances and rivalries in the patterns of kaiju activity. The real answer might be much simpler: perhaps kaiju fight each other because everything else is beneath their notice.

At least, that's how it appears to the military forces that have attempted to kill or drive off these giant monsters. Bullets, missiles, bombs—even advanced weapons, such as lasers and sound-wave generators—either have little effect or are shrugged off completely. When more radical measures are taken, the effects can be nearly as bad as the monster itself: deploying the so-called "oxygen destroyer" superweapon against one of the first known kaiju resulted in decades of ruin for Japan's east coast fishery without permanently eliminating the enormous reptile.

DECIMATION of a city by THE KAIJU.

Hippocampus

Noble sea horse

They are some of the most beautiful creatures of the world's oceans, beasts with the strength of the tides and the grace of the waves. Their graceful "manes" of shimmering membrane throw off sparkling cascades of sea foam as they leap and buck in the surf, the sleek blue-green of their fine scales flashing in the sunlight. They are the steeds of the sea folk and the warhorses of the water gods, drawing the chariot of Neptune through his deep domain. They are the legendary sea horses, the majestic *hippocampi*.

In the most basic terms, a hippocampus is half horse and half fish. But the sea horse is so much more than a simple hybrid. Its horse-like forequarters are of enormous size and strength, as large as those of a heavy draft horse but much sleeker, and its front legs end in clawed, webbed fins, rather than hooves. The sharp teeth in its long jaws are similar to a dolphin's, its large round eyes have a transparent second eyelid allowing it to see underwater, and, where a horse has a mane, the hippocampus has a long, spiny dorsal fin. The scaled hindquarters of the hippocampus are more like those of a *sea serpent* (p. 104) than an ordinary fish: a powerful tail, 15 feet or more in length, ending in a broad flipper with which the sea horse propels itself through the water. Coloration ranges through all the shades of the sea, from dark blues and greens to pale pearl tones, with the front end of the beast generally a lighter shade than the rear. Hippocampi have both gills and lungs.

Hippocampi are intelligent but temperamental, much like dry-land wild horses. Although most tribes of *merfolk* (p. 90) make use of hippocampi as mounts and draft animals, to suggest that sea horses have been "domesticated" is inaccurate; their relationship is more one of mutual agreement, which perfectly suits the free-spirited temperament of both species. Typical sea cavalry tactics have mer-soldiers, hanging on to harnesses of woven kelp, being pulled into battle by swift sea horses. Once combat commences, the hippocampi—which are often partially armored by breastplates of shell and coral—fight in the front line, while the mer-soldiers harry the enemy with long lances, tridents and nets. Water chariots, though impressive, are not normally used in warfare but are reserved mainly for ceremonial occasions.

The hippocampus is found worldwide, and many dry-land cultures have adopted the sea horse as an emblem of Earthly power—the horse symbolizing military control on land, the sea serpent symbolizing mastery of the oceans. Every now and then, some would-be hero attempts to make his name by capturing and breaking a hippocampus. These attempts end, almost exclusively, in spectacular drownings.

Sea Serpent

Deadly coils of the deep

We name our planet Earth, but it should more accurately be called "Water"—after all, oceans cover 70 percent of its surface. And beneath those hundreds of millions of square miles of waves, the black reaches of the sea hold secrets we've only begun to realize. Here lie the domains of the *merfolk* (p. 90) and their kin, as well as the darker, older things told of in ancient mariners' tales. Down here, the mighty *sea serpents* writhe, their immense coils gliding silently through the deeps.

The sea serpent is known to science only through witness reports, from fragmentary remains washed up on beaches and evidence of their attacks—no live specimen has been captured or observed at length. Though limbless and snake-like, they are thought to be related to terrestrial dragons, and, like dragons, sea serpents exhibit wide variations in size and appearance. The largest specimens credibly witnessed have been estimated to stretch more than 200 feet, but enormous individuals of literally biblical proportions—Leviathan of the Book of Revelations is commonly depicted as a sea serpent—appear in legends worldwide.

Sea serpents have been a known danger to shipping since humans first ventured out across the waves. The great serpents attack ships in the same way they subdue whales (the staple of their diet), in the manner of familiar constrictor snakes on land. The serpent rises out of the waves, wraps its huge coils around its target and begins to squeeze and roll, crushing timbers and buckling plating, tossing crew and cargo into the sea. It has been reported that some larger sea serpents are also able to create an intense local whirlpool by swimming in fast circles around a target ship, dragging it under the water.

Some smaller individuals can be discouraged from their attack by irritants such as gunfire and flares, but it's best to avoid serpent attention altogether. Conservative dumping practices provide less of a trail for the monsters to follow, and staying away from the whale migration routes in which sea serpents hunt can further reduce the danger. But any old salt will readily remind you of the best defense against not only sea serpents but all kinds of marine disaster: strict observance of the many shipboard rituals and taboos, the superstitions sea sailors have sworn by since ancient times.

Aspidochelone

The island turtle

The dark, deep oceans of our word are the domain of giants—not just massive mundane creatures such as whales and giant squid, but also *sea serpents* (p. 104) and other, older horrors it doesn't pay to think about too much. But of all the seas' giants, few are as massive as the slow-moving, long-living creature known to the Greeks as the *aspidochelone*, the island turtle.

The aspidochelone—also known as the *zaratan* in the Middle East—is by far the largest of the Chelonian order of reptiles. The shell of an ancient (more than 500 years old) aspidochelone can measure almost 765 yards in length. Unlike its smaller cousins, the vicious hawksbill and snapping turtles, this giant is a peaceful grazer of the oceans. With only its shell breaking the surface of the water, the enormous turtle swims along with its vast jaws wide open as pheromone-like chemicals in its saliva attract whole schools of fish into its mouth. When it has gathered a mouthful, it slams shut the gates of its jaw and swallows then repeats the process thousands of times over during the course of its uneventful centuries-long lifespan.

This peaceful, mindless routine is broken only by mating season, which comes once every century, or so, depending on global climate trends and the periodic arrival of humans. So massive is the aspidochelone, and so seldom does it dive, that over the years, trees and other vegetation take root and thrive in the soil and debris accumulated on the creature's shell. Sailors who mistake the tree-lined hump of the aspidochelone's vast back for an island often come "ashore" in search of game and fresh water. The island turtle doesn't mind this tromping about on its shell; it takes a lot of stimulus to get an aspidochelone's attention. But if the sailors provide that stimulus by lighting a painful fire on the thing's back, the great turtle will dive in an attempt to relieve the irritation, dragging the sailors—and possibly their ship—into the depths with it.

Aspidochelone have no natural predators, although they do have an impressive collection of parasites gathered around them. Their only real threat comes from human activity—collisions with ships and poisoning or depletion of their food supply. Even worse is the threat of global climate change; changing temperature patterns disrupt their long breeding cycles, and rising sea levels wash out egg-laying sites.

Mishipizhiw

Northern water cougar

From the headwaters of the Athabasca River to the lowest reaches of the Great Lakes, those who know the lakes and rivers of northern North America—today's recreational canoeists, the fur traders before them and the Native peoples before them—know to watch out for strange currents in the water. An odd ripple on an otherwise smooth lake or an unusual eddy in raging white water might be a sign of a hidden obstacle...or something far worse. For, in these northern waters lurks the *mishipizhiw*, the dreaded water cougar, and many unwary travelers have been dragged down by the coils of its saw-toothed tentacle-like tail.

Though mishipizhiw is called "water cougar," "great lynx" or "night panther," it isn't a true feline, nor even a mammal, though its general body shape—powerful rear swimming legs, clawed front feet and blunt, fanged muzzle—give a cat-like impression. The creature's jaw is loose-hinged, like that of a snake, enabling it to open its mouth wide enough to swallow its prey whole. From the nape of its neck to the tip of its tail, the mishipizhiw's spine is studded with wicked spikes that resemble the teeth of a ripsaw. As well as snaring the mishipizhiw's victims, this long and muscular tail can also stir up sucking whirlpools in calm lakes and temporarily alter the current of all but the most fast-flowing rivers.

A *manitou*, or spirit creature, the mishipizhiw, though a savage and merciless predator, must not be regarded as evil or malevolent; it lives, and kills, according to the natural order of things. In fact, if addressed with respect and given the proper offerings—good, aromatic tobacco or well-tanned hides are a safe bet—the mishipizhiw will not only leave a traveler in peace but can even assist his journey by granting him swift, favorable currents.

Monster Fact

As with so much of monster lore, accounts of the mishipizhiw blend—or become confused—with those of creatures in other regions. As one example, the water cougar is sometimes associated with the so-called "Chief of Fishes," a sturgeon of enormous size that protects its smaller relations. Elsewhere, a 17th-century description of an Ojibwa cliff painting by missionary Father Jacques Marquette is said by some to depict a mishipizhiw, though others (including, apparently, Marquette himself) claim it is another monster—the bird-like *piasa*. See p. 172 for the priest's account.

Bunyip

Water monster of Australia

The wildlife of Australia is famously unlike that of any other continent, dominated as it is by that strange pouch-bearing branch of the animal kingdom known as the marsupials and featuring rare monotremes, such as the duck-billed platypus and the hedgehog-like echidna. Australia's monsters are weird and various as well, the most famous being the Bigfoot-like yowie and the ubiquitous aquatic monster known generally as the *bunyip*.

Bunyip are known by dozens of different names around this island continent, and regional variants of the species can display surprising physical diversity. But universal features of physiology, behavior, habitat and diet have led monsterologists to classify the great bulk of Australian water monsters as bunyip. A typical bunyip has a large, seal-like body with a muscular tail, large webbed rear legs and fin-like feet and more delicate front legs ending in webbed talons. Fur is present in varying lengths, often growing as a thick mane around the head and neck and absent at the hindquarters, where scaly skin shows through. The head is described as calf-like or like that of a blunt-muzzled dog, with tusks either straight like a walrus' or curved like a boar's.

The bunyip dwells in shallow waters—creeks, ponds and billabongs (oxbows)—where it spends most of its time under water, eating plants and fish and coming up only occasionally for air. As is typical for an Australian animal, the bunyip are marsupials, their pouch-bound young breathing from an air bubble their mother has trapped in her pouch and which is replenished when she surfaces herself to breathe.

Bunyip aggressively protect their territory, especially when their young first venture out of their protective pouch. Humans approaching a bunyip cub on the shore, or even simply walking past when a cub is near, risk attack. The parent bunyip (mother or father) will explode out of the water and attempt to drag the trespasser down to drown. Running away from the water isn´t a sure escape route, because the amphibious bunyip is surprisingly fast on dry land. Climb a tree or, better yet, simply avoid Australian shorelines during the October-to-November calving season.

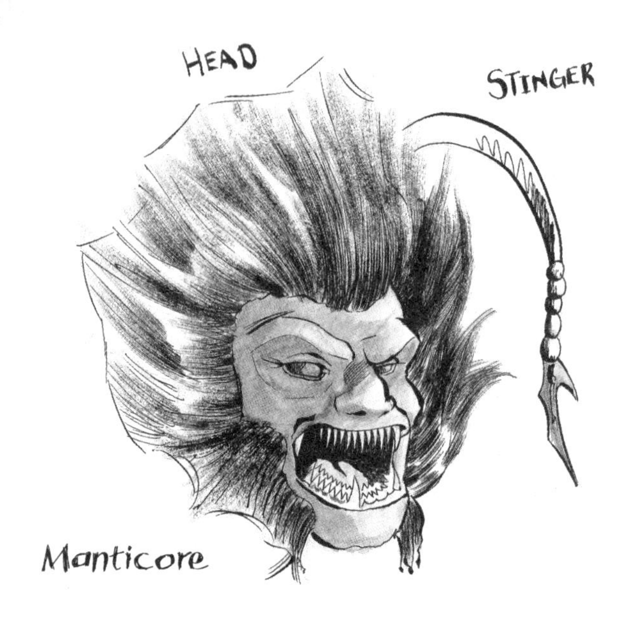
HEAD
STINGER
Manticore

Dobharchú

Chapter 4:
Animal- and Plant-like Monsters

Ever get the feeling you were being watched as you walked through the woods? Chances are, you probably were; the world has no shortage of spirits, monsters and humanoids of the forest who have a vested interest in keeping an eye on trespassers.

Dragon

King of the monsters

Bound securely to an old, charred wooden post, rusty red with blood from decades or even centuries of use, a trembling young woman awaits her fate. She knows why she's here, knows she must give up her life so that her people might survive, but that knowledge doesn't keep her from trembling, doesn't keep the tears from streaming down her face. She can hear the monster coming through the forest—the crack of saplings being crushed and the deep vibrations of its heavy footsteps. She can smell its brimstone breath. At last, with a crash of foliage, it lumbers into the clearing where she's chained. Red-gold and huge, snake-skinned and bat-winged, the horned head at the end of its snake-like neck showing huge, fang-filled jaws that ooze smoke and drip glowing cinders: this is the *dragon*.

There's not a corner of the world that doesn't have at least one variety of dragon stalking its forests and wastelands. Throughout recorded history and as far back as prehistoric times, people on every continent (with the possible exception of Antarctica) have dealt with these monstrous reptiles. In fact, it's no stretch to say that, of all living creatures on Earth, only the domestic dog is more universally associated with humans. And like dogs, dragons come in an almost limitless variety of physical shapes: winged or wingless; big as houses or small as housecats; long and snaky or stout and bullish; living on mountaintops or living on the seafloor; fire-breathing or not.

With some exceptions (*lung*, p. 118), dragons are vicious creatures of chaos and evil, hungry for humans and their livestock. They are also generally quite stupid, though it has been demonstrated that the intelligence of some dragon species is tied to the individual's age. A dragon of ancient years might be a genius by human standards and will have used its long life to gather fabulous treasure and great magical knowledge. Smart or not, all dragons are extremely dangerous, and none will ever quite lose its taste for human flesh—especially that of young women. Reports of villages, and even whole kingdoms, held hostage by dragons demanding regular sacrifices are all too familiar in the history of monster-human relations.

Slaying a dragon is a legendarily difficult task. The safest way to go about it is through the use of magic or some kind of trap. But dragons are notoriously resistant to spells, and even the most dim-witted have a wariness and cunning that makes them frustratingly difficult to trick or snare. Attacking all but the smallest dragons through physical combat is almost suicidal. Dragon-hide is generally as tough as steel, and unless would-be slayers know of a weak point, such as a missing scale on the underbelly, their only hope of winning the encounter is to go for the eyes and hope they get lucky. A dragon-slayer's career is generally quite short.

Chimera

Three-headed monstrosity

It's interesting to note the number of monsters that haunt our vocabulary. A person who financially or emotionally drains those close to them is often referred to as a "vampire." Someone who has overcome great personal obstacles is often said to have "slain his dragons" or "overcome her demons." "Frankenstein" is used in a number of ways, none of them good. The word *chimera* has entered the language, too: *Webster's* gives one definition for chimera as "an illusion or fabrication of the mind, especially an unrealizable dream." As anybody who knows monsters will tell you, that's a pretty gentle definition for one of the most grotesque monstrosities that ever walked the Earth.

The Greek writer Apollodorus, in the second century BC, gave us a description a little closer to the truth. "It was," he writes, "a single being that had the force of three beasts, the front part of a lion, a tail like a dragon and the third head was that of a goat, through which it breathed out fire." The chimera is not a neat and tidy hybrid of three creatures but appears to be some kind of hideous genetic accident. That tail isn't just *like* a dragon's, it *is* a dragon's, a snaky neck with a fanged head. The beast's legs, lion in "front" and goat in "back," face in opposite directions, and the fire-breathing goat's head projects from the middle of the creature's back—often accompanied by another pair of goat legs, uselessly flailing in the air. And not only is it horrible to look at—it stinks, too.

As ugly as the chimera is, its disposition is even uglier. A chimera on the loose is a one-creature plague, rampaging across the countryside killing huge numbers of livestock to feed its monstrous appetite. When it has finally had its fill of sheep and cows—and shepherds and cowboys—it keeps on killing, seemingly for the fun of it, leaving the corpses mauled and uneaten. And while it's decimating the herds, it wipes out acres of fields and orchards with its flaming breath. The chimera has been called "the most monstrous of monsters," and it's certainly one of the top contenders for that title.

The good news is that it doesn't possess any magical or supernatural defenses. It's not immortal, it's not indestructible, it won't teleport away or regenerate its heads. As big and tough as it is, it's a physical creature that can be killed by something—or someone—sufficiently bigger and tougher. For example, the great Greek monster slayer Bellerophon, with the famous flying horse Pegasus, once took out a chimera by weakening it with arrows before stabbing its goat head in the mouth with a special lead-tipped lance. The heat of the monster's fire melted the lead and caused the beast to suffocate.

Lung

Dragon of the Orient

With a few exceptions—and more misconceptions—the *dragons* of the West (p. 114) are generally monstrous in the worst sense of the word, malicious and hostile to humanity. Quite the opposite is true in China and other areas of the Orient, where dragons—in Chinese, *lung*—are celestial beings, benevolent protectors of humanity and symbols of (and fierce warriors for) righteousness and prosperity.

The name "lung" is an overall term for a vast number of species and subspecies of these creatures, which can be startlingly different from each other. In general, however, the Oriental dragon has a long, snake-like scaled body and neck, with lizard-like legs and feet sporting huge claws. Lung are generally four-toed, though dragons of high rank and those associated with royal houses have five digits. The head is vaguely horse-like, with branching or spiraling horns, long whiskers, enormous ears and a flowing beard. Although they seldom have wings, lung can fly, and they move through water with complete freedom. Lung can change their size and shape and become invisible at will, and some species are able to breathe flames, as Western dragons do, while others can emit chilling mists, great winds or poisonous vapors.

Lung have an affinity for water, and the coloration of each species often indicates its particular specialty. Red dragons, for example, are known to be responsible for freshwater lakes and summer heat waves, and black dragons are the guardians of mossy wetlands and dark swamps. Yellow dragons are great scribes and serve as messengers between Earth and the gods, and blue dragons are wise in the ways of healing. All lung are savage fighters in the battle against evil and bear a special hatred for demons and unnatural monsters.

Along with the *feng-hwang* (p. 182), the *k´i-lin* (p. 138) and the tortoise, the Oriental dragon is one of the Celestial Beings of Chinese cosmology and has guided and protected humanity since the beginning of time.

Mokele-mbembe

Lost dinosaur of the Congo

The rivers, lakes, swamps and jungles of the Congo lowlands are the very definition of what was once called "Darkest Africa." Dense to the point of impassability, unspeakably hot and treacherously wet, the land teems with strange and dangerous creatures: leopards, gorillas, elephants, buffalo, chimpanzees, mambas, pythons, crocodiles, hippopotami, termites, ants, malaria-bearing mosquitoes and the deadly tsetse fly. It's a land that holds secrets, and one of the strangest of these is the amphibious monster known as "That Which Stops Rivers": *mokele-mbembe*.

The mokele-mbembe is an imposing reptilian beast. Its scaly body is as big as an elephant's, with a long tail and neck that triple the body length. The tail is heavy and muscular, and the flexible neck ends in an almost comically tiny head. The legs are relatively short and stout, ending in flat, spade-clawed feet that leave tracks more than three feet wide. It inhabits swamps, lakeshores and the shallows of rivers, spending most of its time in the water, where its great weight is more easily supported. Although it will attack and kill any creature that harasses it, including humans—the hippopotamus is a particular enemy—the mokele-mbembe is vegetarian, its diet consisting mainly of the succulent malombo plant.

The physical description and dietary habits of this terrifying creature have led many researchers to conclude that the mokele-mbembe is in fact a species of sauropod dinosaur that has somehow survived into modern times. Certainly, its habitat is as close as our world comes to the lush climate of millions of years ago, and if a dinosaur could hide anywhere, the deep jungles of Africa would be the place. So, is mokele-mbembe a dinosaur? The short answer is "sort of, maybe." If the swamp monster is of dinosaur descent, it must have evolved over the thousands of millennia since its ancestors' heyday, adapting to the changed climate and new pressures. Rather than being a "lost dinosaur," it's far more accurate to describe mokele-mbembe as a modern species of an ancient line.

The current status of the mokele-mbembe is unknown. Logging, farming and human settlement continue to push into its once-isolated habitat. Toxic runoff from industrial operations, such as copper mining, in the highlands finds its way into the lowland water supply, with possibly disastrous effects. The jungle is thick with poachers, bandits and trophy hunters, and the region is wracked by war, which is not only lethal to animal and monster life but prevents scientific teams from gathering hard data. The mokele-mbembe, whose ancestors survived millions of years of geological upheaval, might not survive even 100 years of modern mankind.

Salamander

Fire-loving lizard

The range of environments to which life—both mundane and monstrous—has adapted is a constant source of wonder. From the pitch-black ocean depths to the mountain tops and dimensions that exist beyond the normal, living creatures have evolved to thrive in the most inhospitable places. Of these, few have adapted to a habitat as extreme as that of the *salamander*. Unlike the run-of-the-mill amphibian that shares its name and some physical characteristics, the true salamander is never more comfortable than when it's nestled in the heart of a raging fire.

The salamander's fireproofing is the result of several unique physical characteristics. First, its strange body chemistry acts in some ways as a natural refrigerator, preventing the salamander from cooking alive in its fiery environment. Second, the creature's thick hide has a high mineral content, in the form of asbestos-like fibers, providing a natural fireproof heat shield. Third, the salamander continually oozes a milky white gel from its pores and mucous membranes. This gel has a high insulation value, is fiercely flame-retardant and serves to keep the salamander's hide moist, though fire burns around it. Salamander milk also provides the strange little lizard's only physical defense—it's one of the deadliest poisons found in nature.

To look at, the fire-lizard isn't really all that remarkable. It is a small animal (six to eight inches from snout to tail), with a somewhat blunt face and an unusually slimy skin. Coloration is mostly a mottled bright orange and red, with the occasional speckling of yellow, coal black and even blue—campfire camouflage. Its diet is cinders, ash and charred wood, supplemented by occasional grubs, snails and insects found in wood. Salamanders can live for some time outside of fire, but if things get too cool for too long, they will hibernate, for years if necessary, inside hollow trees until a forest fire or human wood burning rouses them. It's not uncommon for opportunistic salamanders to make their homes in chimneys, blacksmith shops and other comfortable places in which fires burn regularly.

Salamanders are harmless and nonaggressive, relying on their natural poison, which is lethal even to touch, and their blazing surroundings to protect them from harm. Because salamander skin protects as well as asbestos, without the health hazards, their hides are in some demand for use in making fireproof clothing. Salamander trappers are usually right behind the firefighters when a forest starts to go up in smoke.

Amphisbaena

Two-headed desert lizard

The scuttling sound of claws on rock and sand isn't uncommon in the deserts of North Africa, where countless species, monstrous and otherwise, hide in the wastelands. But take a closer look at those big lizard tracks, and you might notice something strange—each pair of footprints points in the opposite direction from the other. Follow the tracks to a dark cave or crevice and you're likely to see two pairs of glowing yellow eyes. Two pairs of eyes...but one animal—the bizarre, double-ended reptile known as the *amphisbaena*.

About the size of a small dog or large badger, the scaly amphisbaena is built along standard reptilian lines but with two "front halves" connected in mirror image. The creature's legs are long, powerful and built for speed and end in feet boasting nasty, hooked talons. Its coloration ranges from rusty tan to olive green, and its eyes literally glow, thanks to their natural phosphorescence. Like many reptiles, the amphisbaena has remarkable powers of regeneration; if it's cut in two, the halves will instinctively drag themselves to a safe bolthole and, after a few days of recuperation, are once again fused together. One half alone cannot regenerate.

With its two heads and opposing pairs of feet, the amphisbaena is not only difficult to surprise, it can move rapidly in any direction, making it extremely hard to catch. When moving down-country, it has an even faster mode of transportation—one head takes the other in its mouth, and, tucking in its legs, the amphisbaena forms itself into a hoop to roll rapidly down steep slopes. Should one of these speedy lizards somehow manage to find itself cornered by a hunter, it will fight, attacking in a wolverine-like frenzy of jaws and claws.

Although it is now limited to isolated pockets of the North African wilderness, researchers speculate that the amphisbaena and related reptiles were once far more widespread; tales of two-headed lizards and "hoop snakes" abound in every corner of the globe. It's likely that many of these species, like so many of our monsters, fell victim to over-hunting—the dried and powdered skin of an amphisbaena is a well-known remedy for rheumatism and lung ailments, and live specimens are said to have a beneficial effect on difficult pregnancies.

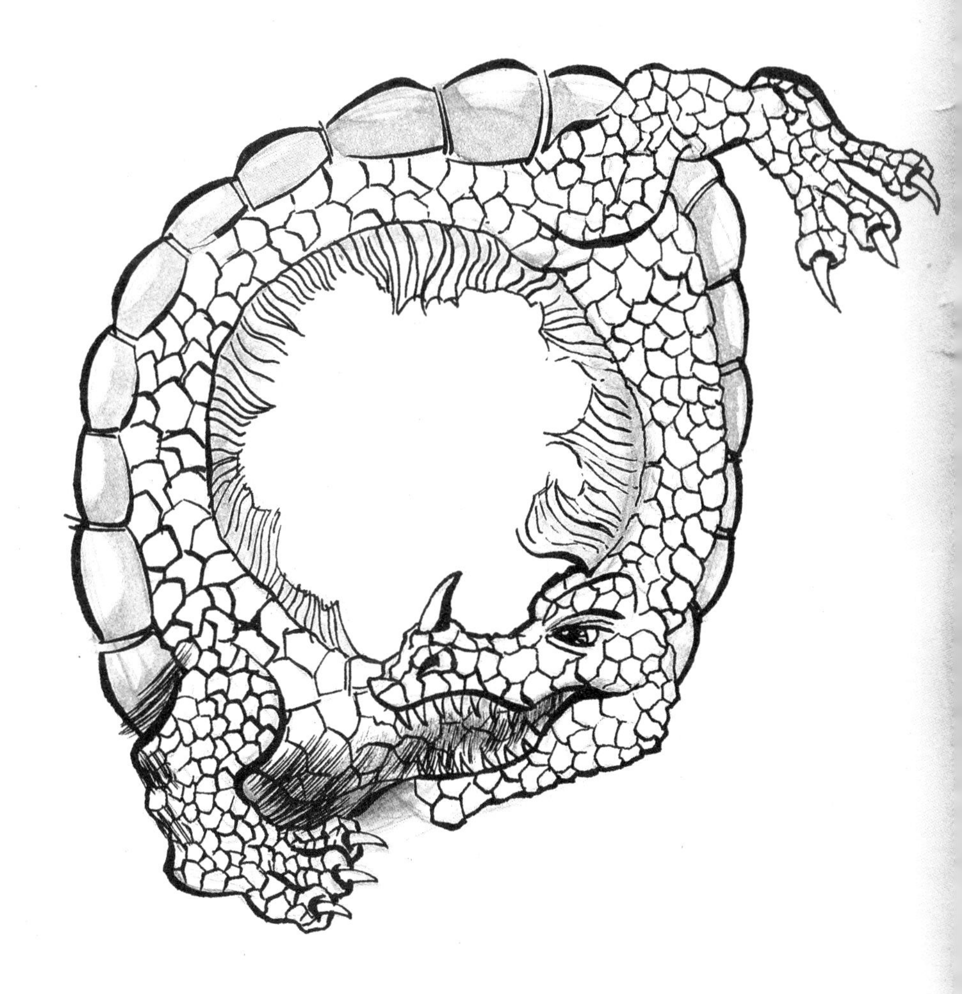

Basilisk

The reptile with paralyzing eyes

With a range straddling Europe and Asia, the *basilisk* is one of the most widely distributed monsters and one of the most famous. From central France to western Mongolia, monster watchers keep their ears open for this strange reptile's distinctive high-pitched "creaking door" call. Spotting the naturally shy basilisk is a rare event.

Adult basilisks are about the size of medium-sized dogs and have a bipedal stance like that of prehistoric theropods or bird-like dinosaurs. They are agile runners, and their smaller foreclaws are as nimble as those of raccoons. Basic coloration ranges from mottled olive to red-brown, and basilisks have a modest chameleon-like ability. Males are more colorful and sport extravagant spiny crests running from the head to the middle of the back. But the most striking feature of the basilisk is its enormous eyes.

The basilisk's eyes, which occupy more than half of its facial area, are the source of the myth that its gaze has the power to turn people to stone. In fact, a unique arrangement of muscular venom sacs in its sinuses allows the basilisk to project a narrow jet of a liquid nerve agent from its highly adapted tear ducts. When this powerful toxin is inhaled, it causes near-instant paralysis. The effect of the basilisk's venom is neither permanent nor lethal.

Basilisks are not generally dangerous to humans. Like coyotes, they are scavengers and opportunistic predators and only use their venom as a means of escape from threats.

The exceptions are if they're disturbed during the height of mating season or if a nest is threatened. In these cases, the enraged basilisks will attack in pack fashion; a solitary basilisk won't attack unless cornered.

Manticore

Poisonous lion creature

If you spend any time studying the monstrous ecology of our world, it's impossible to avoid the eventual question: "What makes human beings so tasty?" Normal carnivores generally go out of their way to avoid human contact, attacking people only when cornered or starving, but a large percentage of monsters crave the taste of human flesh, actively hunting down men, women and children. Some of these monsters are intelligent and evil, motivated by hate, others have magical or mystical reasons for cannibalism, but many are straightforward hunters that happen to take humans as prey. Of these, few are more terrifying than the toxic *manticore*.

Like many monsters native to the Near and Middle East, such as the *sphinx* (p. 134), the manticore's basic body shape is that of a lion. Also like the sphinx, the manticore's face is human-like. The similarities end there. Despite having a red-complexioned human face, the manticore has only animal intelligence, and its gaping mouth is lined with three rows of tiny, needle-like teeth, which it uses to rasp and grind the meat of its victims to shreds. The manticore's paws lack effective claws, but it makes up for this deficiency with a long, articulate tail tipped with a fan of tendrils, each bearing a stinger filled with deadly poison.

The manticore hunts cat-fashion, stalking and hiding until within sprinting distance of its prey, at which point it springs with blinding speed and chases down its target until it is within stinging range. With a whipping motion of its tail, the manticore can shoot its stingers up to 30 yards, and the toxin causes death by cardiac arrest in seconds. The manticore is immune to its own venom; in fact, the manticore requires the toxin for proper digestion and is unable to consume meat that has not been poisoned.

A manticore fed untainted meat will soon die of intestinal hemorrhaging or malnutrition.

The upside of the manticore is that, although it has many magical cousins in the world of monsters, it is not itself supernatural in any way. Its venom has no enchanted properties, its fur won't block bullets, its gaze won't hypnotize you. It might be frightening, with that leering human face and those idiot animal eyes, but it's no tougher, physically, than the lions its shape makes a mockery of—though that's plenty tough, in itself.

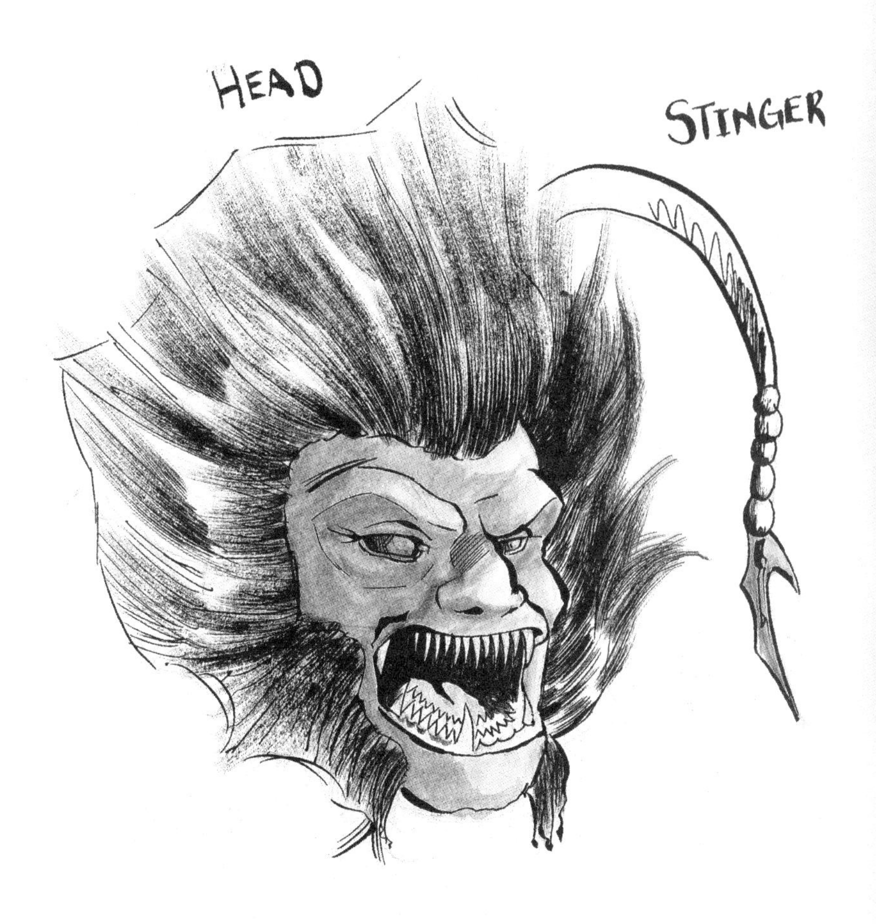

Leucrota

Monster born of lion and hyena

In the vast majority of cases, animals—and monsters—of different species cannot crossbreed. Even when a monster is described as a "cross between" one and another creature, the expression is usually used to denote, say, a bird-like head on a cat-like body, rather than an actual genetic combination of the two creatures. But every rule, even a rule of nature, has its necessary exceptions, and, in this case, the bizarre *leucrota*, the unnatural offspring of a hyena and a lioness, is the best example.

The leucrota isn't a simple blend of the two animals; rather, it seems to reflect a strange set of genetic potentials that lie dormant in the DNA of both species. Its body is donkey-like, with a curling lion's tail, and the head is a blend of lion and hyena features that come across as badger-like. In that head is set one of the strangest jaw structures in nature, hinged near the top of the skull, so that the leucrota's broad grin extends right up to its ears. Rather than teeth, the leucrota has two sharp blades of solid bone, direct extensions of the skull that protrude from its upper and lower jaw. The legs are similar to those of a deer or antelope and end in rather dainty cloven hooves. The leucrota's mysterious mishmash of physical traits also produces some strange limitations: the creature's spine is partially fused and inflexible, rendering the beast incapable of turning its head to look behind or even very far to the sides.

Despite its solid spine, the leucrota is a very speedy, if not very nimble, runner on its graceful legs. It's not quite the fastest of animals, as the Roman historian Pliny reported, but there aren't many running creatures, especially in its native India, that can beat the leucrota on the straightaway. The leucrota won't turn down an opportunity to hunt humans. It gets this opportunity surprisingly often, because its natural cry sounds eerily like a human voice, though it is not intelligent and cannot actually speak. Travelers in the western reaches of India who hear the sound of a man gibbering nonsense in the undergrowth should think twice before investigating.

Monster Fact

As the very rare and unlikely offspring of two species that are themselves threatened, the leucrota is highly endangered and might even be extinct. As long as there are hyenas and lions, though, it's possible for the leucrota to keep coming back.

Yali

The elephant lion of India

Many of Earth's monsters can be seen as holdovers from a time when the continents shook with the footsteps of now-extinct giants. The dinosaurs are obvious candidates for monsterhood, and their survival has been put forward as an explanation for all kinds of monstrous activity. But we don't even have to go that far back. Well into relatively modern times—say, 200,000 years ago—the earth teemed with giant mammals as weird as any monster. Of these, only a few, such as the fearsome *yali* of India, survive.

Imagine a lion the size of an elephant and you've got the basic idea of the unstoppable predator that is the yali. As much as 10 feet high at the shoulder, the yali's shaggy-haired, tawny body is bulky but unmistakably feline, with retractable claws up to a foot long on all four paws. Its head is more elephant than feline, with a mouthful of fangs and a short trunk. The trunk is stubbier and less flexible than that of a true elephant, and it might be an evolutionary holdover; the yali doesn't grasp or manipulate with its trunk but uses it only during mating rituals and to sniff the air in all directions. Males also boast a pair of curving, pointed tusks, which are used in battle for courtship rights.

Unlike elephants, yali are carnivorous—in fact, elephants are its preferred prey. Although yali live in small prides, like lions, they don't hunt in packs; a solitary yali can stalk and kill an elephant on its own. Its method of hunting, however, is classically feline: slow stalking from downwind, then a pounce onto its victim's back with all fours. The yali overbears its target, toppling the elephant off its feet and gripping its back with its forepaws, while it rips and tears with its rear claws and gouges, when it can, with its tusks. The kill is shared with the pride, the alpha male getting first dibs on the meat.

Although it has survived tens of thousands of years from prehistoric times, the yali in two centuries has gone from being very rare to critically endangered. Thanks to deforestation and urbanization, yali numbers in the wild might be down to a few dozen. Soon, the only way to see yali will be in the carvings in Indian and Sri Lankan temples, in which the giant predators symbolize man's animal passions.

Sphinx
Ancient riddling guardian

> What has one voice but goes four-footed in the morning, two-footed in the afternoon and three-footed in the evening?
>
> —The riddle of the Theban Sphinx

Of all the hybrid man-animals of North Africa, the Middle East and the Mediterranean, the species of lion-bodied *sphinx* are the most common and the most various: they are a textbook example of monstrous dispersal and evolution. The most ancient species, the sphinxes of Egypt, were of three types: the human-headed *androsphinx*, the ram-headed *criosphinx*, and the hawk-headed *heiracosphinx*. Of these, only the androsphinx has survived to modern times. As the sphinx spread into the Middle East, certain populations, either through evolution or interbreeding with other monsters, developed semi-functional wings and a predominantly female sex balance, becoming difficult to distinguish from the physical form of the celestial *lamassu* (p. 166).

The most widely known species, however, is the classical sphinx of Greece. The largest of sphinxes, it has the body of a huge lion, a serpent's tail and the head and face of a human. The Greek sphinx also sports wings, but, like those of its Middle Eastern cousins, they are inadequate for sustained flight and useful only for controlled glides and long leaps. Of these sphinxes, the most notable was the Theban Sphinx, an ancient female that once took up residence near the city of Thebes and gleefully devoured travelers who failed to answer correctly her now-famous riddle. The creature was eventually dispatched when the tragic hero-king Oedipus presented her with the solution.

This riddling behavior is the defining social characteristic of the sphinxes. Like most man-animal hybrids of the region, such as the *lamassu* and *shedu* (p. 166) and the *scorpion men* (p. 58), sphinxes are guardian creatures that watch over bridges, narrow passes and other travel choke points. Unlike these other hybrids, however, a sphinx seldom has a holy or sacred reason for guarding its spot. Rather, it seeks out these places for its own sport: the pleasure of riddling and the joy of killing the unworthy.

Unicorn

Magical one-horned forest creature

A bright shape glimpsed on a distant hill, a flash of white in the depths of a wood—that is all most people can hope to see of the fabulous unicorn, and, even then, the odds are long. Elusive and reclusive, this rare magical beast shuns all (well, almost all; see below) contact with coarse, brutish humanity, preferring to stay hidden in deep forests and woodland glades.

One place to find unicorns in great numbers is on the coats of arms and banners of noble families and royal houses, their presence symbolizing purity and strength. This popular image of the unicorn—a powerful, white horse with one golden horn—is a bit misleading. In reality, unicorns have more in common with goats than with horses. Generally smaller than a horse, standing about as tall as a medium-sized pony, the unicorn is bearded and shaggy, sporting tufts of hair at its knees and around its hooves. Western European unicorns are exclusively white, with a long, twisted horn of yellowed ivory, but variations in color and shape appear farther to the south and east. Some North African unicorns, for example, are reported to have black and even red coats, and in Russia and the Near East, unicorns bear forked horns. By the time the traveler reaches India and East Asia, true unicorns are almost entirely displaced by such similar local species as the flying *k'i-lin* (p. 138).

The most distinctive feature of a unicorn is, of course, its famous horn, which is used for attack and defense. Driven by the unicorn's powerful muscles, the horn can easily penetrate even elephant hide, and the beast is nimble enough to use its wicked weapon to parry human hunters' spears and swords. The horn has magical properties, too, which is probably why those hunters are there in the first place. The beautiful ivory spike can purify toxic water and spoiled food and renders anyone holding it immune to all poison and disease. Unicorn horn is a key ingredient in countless love potions and elixirs of immortality. Over-hunting for the horn trade is largely responsible for the unicorn's extreme rarity in all but the most remote corners of Europe.

You might wonder how human hunters manage to corner and kill a powerful, lightning-fast beast that can sense danger a mile off. Unfortunately, the unicorn has—like so many monsters—a well-known weakness for beautiful young maidens. Unlike more vicious creatures, the unicorn doesn't mean the girl any harm; it is drawn hypnotically by her aura of goodness and purity. The poor love-struck creature will walk right up to a maiden set as bait and lay its head in her lap, allowing spearmen to kill it at their leisure. The only thing the hunters have to worry about is the possibility of their human "bait" luring a less-gentle creature of the forest....

K'i-lin

The transcendent Chinese unicorn

This book is a guide to "monsters of the world," so it might be a bit of a stretch to include the *k'i-lin*, the so-called Chinese unicorn, in its pages: this noble creature isn't so much "*of* the world" as "*above* the world"—in both the spiritual and the physical senses. Beings of great wisdom and pure goodness, the ancestors of the k'i-lin long ago evolved beyond the needs of the material world, and the species now dwells almost exclusively in the spiritual dimension known to the Chinese as "heaven." The presence of a k'i-lin in the physical world is a once-in-a-generation event of great significance.

In their native realm, the k'i-lin are indescribable beings of pure light and spiritual energy. When they descend to Earth, their form is that of a hybrid creature with a long, deer-like body, delicate hooves, the tail of an ox and the head of a dragon with a long, flowing lion's mane and a single blunt horn. The k'i-lin is often depicted with dragon-like scales on its body, but this is actually an illusion created by the multicolored pattern of the creature's soft, fine fur. The k'i-lin's horn is soft and fleshy, because this advanced being has no need for physical defense. Indeed, the k'i-lin is nonviolent and refuses to harm any living thing—when it walks, it walks on air inches above the ground to avoid damaging the grass and insects beneath its hooves. The horn does, however, serve as a focus for the k'i-lin's great magical powers, which are nothing short of miraculous.

Encountering—or even glimpsing—a k'i-lin is an extremely rare event, a great honor and a powerful good-luck charm. The k'i-lin only descend to our world on two occasions: one is to herald the birth of a child destined to become a great philosopher and to present it with gifts and blessings; the other is to acknowledge the ascent to the throne of an emperor of perfect wisdom and enlightenment. Because China is now a republic, it may be a long time before another visitation occurs. It has also been suggested that the k´i-lin will return when a great evil force threatens the world. When you consider the enormous evils that have been committed on Earth and the fact that no cavalry of celestial unicorns has shown up, you should have some idea of how seriously the k´i-lin take their separation from the mundaneworld.

Monster Fact

The k´i-lin is one of the four Celestial Creatures of Chinese philosophy, along with the *lung* (p. 118), the *feng-hwang* (p. 182), and the *gui xian*, or cosmic tortoise. Each of these four species bears responsibility for one of the cardinal directions of the compass, with the k´i-lin being the rulers and symbols of the Celestial West.

Kelpie

Demonic water horse of Scotland

When the creeks and kills of the rugged Scottish landscape are flooding, moving cross-country can be slow and frustrating for a traveler on foot. Miles of distance and hours of travel can be added by the search for an intact bridge or suitable ford. You can imagine, then, the temptation when one comes across a docile and accommodating stallion, already bridled, grazing by the riverside. Simply hop on the horse's back and let the powerful animal carry you across, right?

Well, maybe, if you're foolish or a stranger to those parts. A wise Scotsman would walk far out of his way to avoid that sleek black pony. Anyone getting on the steed's back would more than likely receive, instead of a dry crossing, a hideous death by drowning under the claws and hooves of the dark *kelpie*, one of the most feared and formidable freshwater monsters. Known in Gaelic as *each uisge*, or water horse, the kelpie is an utterly evil and vicious faerie, a sadistic creature that takes great pleasure in the suffering of its victims.

Although it might appear as a horse, or even a beautiful young human, the kelpie is not a true shape-shifter. Instead, it casts an illusion, or glamour, to fool mortal eyes. This illusion can be lifted by various magical means and by people with the gift of "second sight." The kelpie's true form is a two-legged horse-thing, a twisted parody of human and horse with shaggy, midnight-black hair and a wild mane and tail that flow and whirl like rushing black water. Where a stallion's forelegs would be are two strong, gnarled arms that end in wicked, three-fingered claws. Its mouth is filled with sharp fangs, rather than the blunt teeth of a horse, and its eyes burn with hate.

Escaping from a kelpie is quite impossible: any body part that touches the vile beast is stuck fast, until the water horse has thoroughly enjoyed your death and releases you to drift off down the river. Legends exist of people of great virtue or resourcefulness overcoming the kelpie to claim its bridle—a magical object of unspecified powers—but, unless you're a saint or a hero, your best bet is to stay well away from any suspiciously handy horses in the Highlands.

Yale

Stag of the East

The relationship between the world's monster species and the chivalric knights of the Middle Ages can be quite contradictory, if not outright hypocritical. One of the great ironies of monsterology is that the creatures most admired for their virtues and adopted as symbols of great noble houses—*unicorns* (p. 136), *dragons* (p. 114) and *manticores* (p. 128), for example—were also the creatures most sought after by hunting parties seeking glory and trophies. One such monster, hunted for sport near to the point of extinction, was the fantastic Stag of the East, the mighty *yale*.

The yale, at first glance, appears to be an enormous deer or elk, but the resemblance is superficial. Its body is built along goat-like lines, scaled up to the size and solidity of a heavy draught horse. Its coat is somewhat shaggy, and its coloration reflects the yale's geographic distribution: the Persian plains yale tends toward pale tawny brown, whereas the Indian yale sports a darker, dappled coat that provides camouflage in its forest habitat. Although the yale is a herbivore, it has big, tusked jaws. The head is large and broad, to properly anchor the powerful muscles that bear the creature's long, thick antlers.

These antlers are the yale's claim to fame and its principal means of defense. Unlike the fixed antlers of other horned animals, the yale's antlers can swing and swivel in any direction, from straight forward to straight back, enabling the creature to defend itself against attacks from all sides. Using its neck muscles and the muscles attached to the horns themselves, the yale can swing an antler with enough power to crack solid oak or dent steel. To protect their young, a group of yale—yale travel in small family gatherings, rather than herds—forms a circle, creating an impenetrable wall of antlers and tusks. Females as well as males bear antlers, though the doe's are shorter and do not branch like the stag's.

For the knights of Europe, the yale was a symbol of steadfastness and solid defense, and yale heads and antlers became sought-after decorations for the halls of their castles and manors. With steel armor, lances, warhorses and squads of men-at-arms, medieval nobles took long hunting trips into the Asian wilderness, slaughtering recklessly. More commonly, though, they simply bought a trophy from an Eastern merchant and told tall tales about its capture. Either way, the result was a world with more yales on royal banners and crests than in the wild.

Catoblepas

Heavy head and deadly eyes

> Obese, downhearted, wary, I do nothing but feel under my belly the warm mud. My head is so heavy that I cannot bear its weight. I wind it slowly around my body; with half-open jaws, I pull up with my tongue poisonous plants dampened by my breath. Once, I ate up my forelegs unawares.
>
> No one, Anthony, has ever seen my eyes; or else, those who have seen them have died. If I were to lift my eyelids, my pink and swollen eyelids, you would die on the spot.
>
> —Gustave Flaubert, *The Temptation of Saint Anthony* (1874)

The *catoblepas*, at first glance, is a formidable creature. The size of a buffalo, its black body bulges with muscle under a thick hide. Its squat legs, adapted to bear its bulk, are powerful and end in heavy, elephantine feet tipped with three hard, spade-like nails used for tearing up the swamp vegetation on which it feeds. Its massive head is tusked and hog-like but hidden under a thick mane of coarse hair that falls over its eyes and muzzle, straggling down into the mud and bog in which it lives.

Those piggy eyes hidden under that shaggy veil are two of the most dangerous weapons known in the natural, or supernatural, world: any creature meeting the gaze of the catoblepas is immediately struck dead. How this lethality is accomplished is unknown, and the difficulty in conducting research is obvious. Victims of the catoblepas' death gaze are rare, and the few unfortunates who have been studied show no marks, burns or other injuries. The current theory, involving some type of vague "psychic blast," is no less speculative than the folklore suggesting that the catoblepas is simply ugly enough to cause a heart attack.

But for all its massive size and deadly weaponry, the catoblepas is ultimately more tragic than frightening, and the creature is often used in literature as a symbol of impotent power. Its body is strong, its eyes are lethal... but the neck connecting the two is pitifully weak, preventing the catoblepas from raising its head off the ground. Down it stays, among the muck, weeds and water plants, unable to look up or use its gaze aggressively. Only the foolishly curious, who crouch down and pull aside the catoblepas' screen of matted hair to reveal the beast's deadly little eyes, have anything to fear.

Shuck

Black dog of the British Isles

The lonely moors and rolling hills of the English countryside, so often postcard-perfect in the light of day, are seldom so charming in the dead of night. Fog and mist chill the bones; meandering country lanes, lovely for strolling in the sunshine, become dark and twisted paths in the pale light of a cloud-covered moon. Tangled hedges whisper their secrets, as the wind whips up and the air becomes electric before the brewing storm. It's on nights like these that travelers must beware one of the most sinister and most common of English demons, the malevolent, midnight-black *Shuck*.

Also known as the Black Dog, Demon Dog, Skriker, Barguest and various other names—Shuck is most commonly used in the region of East Anglia—the beast is generally described as a huge, shaggy-haired, mastiff-type dog, as big as a donkey or medium-sized pony. It appears out of the darkness, its saucer-sized eyes like glowing fireballs, hellishly growling and snarling. The Shuck rarely attacks outright; instead, its manner is more that of a ferocious but well-trained guard dog. Snarling and barking its challenge, it stands its ground and drives trespassers away through sheer terror. For this reason, many consider Shucks to be guardians of sacred places, and some contend that a nerve-wracking encounter with the huge demon dog is actually in one's favor, that, by blocking a traveler's path, the Shuck keeps him away from a greater danger further along the way.

Not all encounters with Shucks take place on the road, however. One of the most famous Black Dog encounters took place on August 4, 1577, in the parish church of Bungay, near Norwich. As reported by Abraham Fleming in a widely circulated pamphlet of the time, a thunderstorm of incredible intensity wracked the village, and, as the frightened people prayed for deliverance, a huge black dog, wreathed in flame and with glowing eyes, appeared in the church. It rampaged through the terrified faithful, killing two and leaving one man withered and crippled, before racing up onto the roof and vanishing into the crashing storm. "This is a wonderful example of God's wrath," Fleming writes, "no doubt to terrify us that we might fear him for his justice."

The Beast of Bungay and a few similar attacks aside, the Shuck is generally terrifying yet harmless, if left unmolested. In any encounter with one of these hellhounds, it's best to do what it obviously wants you to do—run away and stay away. Along with the damage done by its powerful claws and jaws, a Shuck provoked into combat can also inflict terrible burns and muscle spasms; those who are foolish enough to fight with one generally do not have open-casket funerals.

Kitsune

Japan's tricky werefox

Every region of the world has its "trickster" species: a monster or spirit, usually a shape-shifter, primarily concerned with deception, confusion and practical jokes. Most regions, in fact, have more than one, and many are described elsewhere in this guide. In Japan, the trickster niche is filled by the *kitsune*, a lively, intelligent, curious, mischievous—and grudge-holding—species of *werefox*. Every corner of that spirit-haunted nation has its own stories of human encounters with these capricious creatures, but whether the accounts are romantic or sinister, serious or hilarious, the moral is usually the same: don't mess with the kitsune.

It's important to point out that, unlike the werewolves of Europe and elsewhere, the kitsune are *not* humans who have been cursed (or blessed) with the ability to assume the shape of a fox. Some kitsune are trapped souls that have been doomed to werefox form until some condition is met—these conditions range from something as concrete as having a certain holy relic returned to a specific shrine to something as insubstantial as finding a truly pious man. The second, much more common type of kitsune is a fox that has lived long enough to gain the powers of shape-shifting and human speech. These kitsune grow extra tails as they become older, wiser and more powerful. Kitsune can live for several hundred years, leading some radical monsterologists to speculate that all kitsune are of the first type, some of whom have grown so old that they've forgotten their original purpose.

Above all, kitsune are pranksters, dedicated to the cause of social upset and ironic justice. They love to see the proud brought low by the source of their pride and just as dearly love to see the humble elevated by the cause of their humility. Their shape-shifting abilities aren't limited to fox and human shapes, and they can adjust their mass at will. These abilities are a source of endless amusement for the kitsune. Taking the form of a single coin that becomes as massive as a chest of silver is a great prank to play on a greedy man, and taking the form of a skinny (but extremely heavy) runt is a wonderful way to shame an arrogant wrestler. Although they disguise themselves, Japanese werefoxes aren't shy. In fact, they seem to love human company—the number of stories told of fox maidens marrying human men is instructive.

Of course, the number of stories ending in misery for the husband is *also* instructive. If you should find yourself entangled with one of the kitsune, just remember what your coach always told you: "Play by the rules and you won't get hurt."

Monster Fact

The popular Japanese noodle dish *kitsune udon* is so-called because the triangle of sweet fried tofu that tops it resembles a fox's ear.

Chupacabras

Puerto Rican goat sucker

As hidden and secretive as monsters can be, they are still more-or-less known quantities. As long as humans have been walking on two legs and rubbing sticks together to make fire, we've shared the planet with them, and our knowledge of supernatural creatures has been passed down through the generations in legends, lore, mythology, scientific research and eyewitness reports. It's not often that a "new" monster comes to light, but that's exactly what happened in and around the Puerto Rican town of Canóvanas in August 1995.

The scene was something out of a nightmare. More than 150 pets and farm animals, mostly goats, were found dead, killed in the night. They weren't eaten or mauled, as would be expected from wild dogs, big cats or other predators—each was drained of blood through small puncture wounds that tapped major veins or arteries. This episode was not the last time this mysterious vampire-thing would strike. By the end of the year, more than 1000 livestock deaths in Puerto Rico were attributed to the creature that came to be known as *el chupacabras*, the goat sucker.

Eyewitness reports have painted a more-or-less consistent picture of "El Chupa." It moves with blinding speed in leaps of amazing height and distance, propelled by kangaroo-like three-toed legs. Its eyes are large red ovals that seem to glow with reflected light, like those of a cat, and its skin is gray. Its five-foot-tall body is monkey-like, with a long row of spines or quills down its back that some researchers theorize are folded wings. It has wicked teeth and a long serpent's tongue in addition to the unknown organ or feeding apparatus that allows it to make its surgically precise punctures. It has been variously described as making "groaning," "shrieking" or "mumbling" sounds, and a sulfuric stench has been associated with it.

Chupacabras activity quickly spread from Puerto Rico to the United States (mainly Florida, Texas and the Southwest) and Mexico, where the frequency and severity of attacks prompted a government investigation—and a thriving Chupa souvenir industry. But it's still not clear what, exactly, this new monster is. Some researchers say it's an extraterrestrial; others claim it must be some kind of secret, genetically engineered experiment that escaped—or was set loose. Whatever it is, the chupacabras has caused millions of dollars of damage to livestock and left hundreds of communities in terror—and its reported range continues to expand.

Leshiye

Malicious Russian forest imp

Those who wander the forests of the Russian taiga, that vast green sea of pine, aspen and birch that stretches for thousands of miles across the face of the world, will encounter many mysteries in that dark wilderness. Coming upon a logged clearing, for example, it is not unusual to find, on one of the stumps, a large pile of food—bread, salt and *kasha*, a sweet pudding made by boiling grains in milk. This offering has been left by the woodsmen for the *leshiye*, a powerful forest spirit that might otherwise take violent exception to the removal of its beloved trees.

As nature spirits, leshiye are as changeable as the weather and the seasons. They appear in a wide variety of forms, depending on their mood: a goat-footed imp similar to the *satyrs* of Greece (p. 60), a towering tree giant, any form of animal or plant, a green-bearded old peasant with eyes of green stone and short horns poking from his mossy hair. The leshiye and its family—the female *lesovika* and little *leshonki*—are master mimics and use this ability to tease and mislead humans. Whether their pranks cause minor discomfort and embarrassment or death and disaster depends on their wildly swinging temper.

The leshiye are fiercely territorial, each one having its own forest "kingdom" in which it rules as lord over all animals and plants. In the spring, when the leshiyes' tempers match the wild weather, they battle each other over their borders, dueling with thunderstorms and floods. In the summer, the leshiye are more concerned with tending their kingdoms and playing cruel pranks on humans. In the winter, the leshiye's personality becomes appropriately cold and cruel, and even its animal subjects fear the icy winds and killing frosts it commands.

The most reliable way of dealing with these mean-spirited forest imps is through bribery, making appropriate offerings when entering each leshiye's territory or taking from the bounty of the forest through hunting, fishing or logging. If the leshiye isn't placated by gifts, the old fairy-defense trick of turning all one's clothes inside-out and backward might work; depending on the creature's mood, it just might be sufficiently amused—or confused—to leave its victim alone.

Monster Fact

One of the leshiye's favorite summertime tricks is to climb a tree and, hiding in its branches, imitate the crying of a baby. At these times, the leshiye is sometimes referred to as a *zuibotschnik*, from the Russian word for "cradle."

Dryad

Beautiful nymph of the woods

Ever get the feeling you were being watched as you walked through the woods? Chances are, you probably were being watched; the world has no shortage of spirits, monsters and humanoids of the forest that have a vested interest in keeping an eye on trespassers. The woods of the world are, in many cases, the last refuges of these beings, their places of power, their final barricade against human expansion. But not many beings' lives are so closely bound to the lives of the trees as those of the beautiful *dryad*.

Dryads are nymphs, female nature spirits who inhabit trees; a dryad spends most of her life merged body and soul with the trunk, leaves, roots and branches of the tree she calls home. On the occasions that she emerges from her tree to take physical form—she'll never wander more than 20 yards—the dryad takes on the appearance of an exceptionally beautiful young woman. Some dryads appear entirely human; others might have leaf-colored hair, bark-brown skin or some other feature showing her tree-ish nature. Dryads can speak with animals, plants and humans, but this communication is generally telepathic in nature—dryads are physically mute.

The dryad's tree is far more than simply a dwelling place, and the bond between nymph and plant is deep and profound. In many ways, the dryad and her tree are one creature, having grown together all their lives. The dryad senses all that her tree senses—moisture, weather, rot and the energies of the Earth—and the tree is aware of everything the dryad experiences when she is mobile. A dryad is essentially immortal, but she also suffers from any harm done to her tree; if the tree dies, the dryad dies with it. Dryads are usually linked to long-lived tree species, such as oaks.

In the sanctity of the bond between dryad and tree lies the nymph´s only real danger to humans; chopping or pruning trees, without first paying respect to the dryad within, or willfully ruining or burning the forest invites all kinds of curses and other mystical trouble. Aside from human loggers, the dryads´ only real "predators" (if they can be called that) are the impulsive *satyrs* (p. 60), who eternally lust after these beautiful and elusive spirits.

Hodag

Spiny predator of the Wisconsin woods

The lumberjacks and surveyors working the forests of Wisconsin in the late-19th century dealt with a lot of hardships and dangers: flash floods, foul weather, wolves, wildcats, bears, bandits—and a whole strange menagerie of North American monsters lurking in the trees. Most of these were, at worst, irritating pests, but one was a real danger, a vicious predator, a horrible man-eating monstrosity...the *hodag*.

At seven feet long from muzzle to tail, often weighing in excess of 200 pounds, the hodag is probably the largest North American predator, unless you count the omnivorous bears. Its body is solid and barrel-like, with stout legs splayed out like a lizard's, though the hodag isn't as close to the ground as an alligator. The head is huge and horned, with powerful crushing jaws and bulbous eyes held on short stalks. The hodag is covered with short, coarse black hair, not much of which can be seen, thanks to the dozens of wicked spikes and spines that stud its body and flanks, down to the tip of its heavy, muscular tail.

Despite its huge size, the hodag can move almost silently through forests and swamps. Like many monsters, the beast prefers the delicate taste of human flesh but will eat anything it can lay its claws on. The first and last warning of the monster's approach given most victims of the hodag is an overpowering stench.

But, as formidable as it is, hunting and killing a hodag is possible, even easy, once you know its habits. Because of the array of spikes on its body, the creature cannot lay down to sleep. Instead, it leans against a tree. Because hodags are violently territorial, the beast usually uses one particular tree regularly. One simply has to find this tree and saw partway through it, and when the hodag leans against it to nap, the monster will tumble, helpless to the ground.

Because of urban encroachment and deforestation, the hodag is extremely rare in its original Wisconsin, Minnesota, range and has been pushed north, west and south over the decades. Signs of hodag activity have been detected as far north as the woods of Ontario, and an unconfirmed sighting near Bend, Oregon, in the late ´60s suggests a greatly extended western range. Whether viable breeding populations have been established in these areas is unknown.

Barometz
The vegetable lamb

> There groweth a manner of fruite as it were gourds, and when it is ripe men cut it a sonder, and men fynde therein a beast as it were of fleshe and bone and bloud,as it were a lyttle lambe without wolle, and men eate the beaste and fruit also, and sure it seemeth very strange.
>
> —Sir John Mandeville, *The Travels of Sir John Mandeville*, c. 1360

The biology of monsters is largely a biology of hybrids, of species that seem to comprise aspects of two or more "normal" animals: humans with horse bodies (p. 56), horses with eagles' wings (p. 168), dragon-goat-lion monstrosities (p. 116) and other, weirder combinations. But rarely does the hybridization get so bizarre as to cross the lines between the kingdoms of life—for animal and plant to blend in one species. The most famous exception to this is the *barometz*, or "vegetable lamb," of Persia and Turkey.

Mandeville's account, above, of a seedpod containing a "lyttle lambe without wolle" is actually a description of the unripened barometz. When the fruit is allowed to ripen, that "little lamb" emerges from its casing complete with a fine coat of golden yellow fleece. The tiny lamb-like creature, up to 18 inches long at full growth, remains attached for life to its flexible stalk, which supports the back half of the creature while it walks around on its forelegs, grazing at the end of its tether. When the vegetable lamb has consumed all the forage in its immediate area, about a six-foot radius, the creature dies of starvation and goes to seed, its woolly hairs drifting off on the wind like poplar fuzz, to sow the next generation of barometz.

As a harvested crop, the barometz is a useful little creature. Its yellow fleece, if shorn before the lamb dies and goes to seed, is fine and easily spun, though not as thick and warm as a true sheep's wool. Barometz linen is an excellent cloth for hot climates. The meat of the barometz, though little can be taken from a single plant-animal, is quite nutritious and very light, in taste and texture more like fish than mutton. Vegetable-lamb farming can be a little dangerous, however: wolves love the taste of barometz flesh and can smell the creatures from miles away. If precautions aren't taken, hungry predators can soon overrun a plantation.

Dobharchú

The King Otter of Ireland

Late on a September evening in 1722 in County Donegal, Ireland, a farmer by the name of McGloughlan went searching for his beloved bride, Grace, who hadn't returned from a morning bathing trip to Lake Glenade. He came across a sight worse than even his panicked imagination could have imagined. Her torn body lay on the shore, and standing over her with bloody claws and muzzle was the enormous water creature that had killed and mangled her: the "king otter," the *dobharchú*.

The dobharchú is otter-like only in its general appearance; in its specifics, it's as different from an otter as a lion is from a housecat. It grows to an astounding five or six feet long (as opposed to a true otter's 2.5 feet), and its webbed paws are tipped with much nastier claws than its smaller cousin. A broad, thick skull anchors jaw muscles of bone-breaking power. The dobharchú's pelt is shorter-haired than that of an otter, leading some people to mistake it as hairless, and its coloration is off-white with a distinctive black, cross-shaped marking that extends up the back and neck and across the shoulders.

All mustelids—a family that also includes badgers and weasels—are carnivorous hunters and scrappy fighters. But the dobharchú is a full-on bloody killer, a predator that stalks dogs, deer and humans and seems to kill as much for pleasure as for food. It hunts in typical water-predator fashion, lurking just beneath the surface of the water. When its prey comes too close to the bank, it launches a lightning-fast attack aimed at dragging the target into the water, where the dobharchú has the advantage. The name, "King of Otters," might be more than a reference to the dobharchú's size, because it has been seen hunting with an "entourage" of half a dozen, or more, of its smaller relatives.

Those brave or skilled enough to hunt the dobharchú—the beasts are too intelligent to be trapped with any success—can make good coin from the sale of their pelts, which are in high demand. As well as being soft to the touch, well insulated and waterproof, a coat of properly tanned dobharchú hide is tough enough to offer its wearer some protection against knives and even small-caliber bullets, at a fraction of the weight and bulk of a synthetic bulletproof vest.

Jackalope

Warrior rabbit of the Western plains

> The Dharma is in this world and we cannot leave awareness of this world to obtain the Dharma. Trying to attain enlightenment without awareness of this world is like seeking a horned rabbit.
>
> —Venerable Master Hui Neng, sixth Patriarch of Ch'an Buddhism (638–713)

Rabbits and hares aren't known for being overly noisy or aggressive; unless they're in pain, most members of the family *Leporidae* keep silent, and all would rather run from danger than stand and fight. Both these rules are excepted by their rare cousin of the American West, the majestic *jackalope*. Jackalopes exhibit a remarkable range of calls and voices, and these "warrior rabbits" are distinguished by the males' formidable natural weaponry: a pair of branching, deer-like antlers.

Jackalopes are generally larger than hares and are more powerfully built, with broader, heavier skulls and hind legs even stronger than a jackrabbit's. Only buck jackalopes sport the species' distinctive antlers, which are shed annually and grow back larger and more elaborate each year. These fearsome weapons are used in combat for mating rights, with buck jackalopes launching themselves at each other on their spring-loaded legs to clash in midair. Although these annual duels are seldom fatal, their violence is such that the crash and clatter of antlers can be heard for miles across their tall-grass prairie habitat.

The noise of battle isn't the only distinctive sound of the jackalope. As many cowboys have discovered, to their embarrassment, the horned rabbits are expert mimics of the human voice and seem to be particularly fond of singing along with campfire songs. When the men get up to investigate the unknown voice singing along from the darkness, the jackalope then causes confusion by mimicking the searchers' calls to each other. Even if a jackalope is clearly spotted, catching it is another matter. These speedy animals can outrun an average pony, and they can go to ground and camouflage themselves perfectly. If cornered, they will attack ferociously, leaping as high as six feet in the air to gore a hunter's face and eyes with their antlers.

Monster Fact

Experienced jackalope hunters know to use whisky as bait. The feisty creatures are extremely fond of strong drink and will lap it up until they fall into a drunken stupor, at which point they're slow enough to catch easily. Although jackalope meat combines the best qualities of venison and rabbit, the animals are far more valuable as trophies—most country saloons west of the Mississippi pay top dollar for a mounted jackalope.

Phoenix

Will-o'-wisp

Chapter 5:

Monsters of the Air

They are symbols of strength and speed, nobility and relentless purpose, the swiftest of airborne hunters, gliding silently over foothills and steppes from their cliff-side nests, diving like lightning on their prey...plus, they look really cool.

Shedu and Lamassu

Winged guardians of ancient Iraq

The peoples of ancient Mesopotamia—the Sumerians, Babylonians, Assyrians and others—were serious about security. Their societies were secured by mankind's first laws and constitutions and their economies by mankind's first accounting systems. They worshipped the goddess Innana, also known as Ishtar, whose power was that of the storehouse, the granary and the vault—the power to protect riches. Guarding their magical knowledge was a system of intricate codes and "gates" that modern mystics still struggle to unlock. And to secure their palaces and holy places, their kings called upon the most powerful guardian creatures of the ancient world—the *shedu* and *lamassu*, winged animals with human faces.

Distantly related to the more-famous *sphinx* (p. 134), shedu and lamassu always appear in pairs, male and female. The male shedu's body is a huge, wild bull, with eagle's wings and three forelegs, and its head is that of a giant man, bearded and crowned. The lamassu has the body of a powerful lion, similarly winged, and the face of a beautiful woman. These creatures are not only enormous and physically powerful, they also have great magical knowledge. They spend much of their very long lives on a spiritual plane of existence and are tied to the Earth and the places they protect by enchanted statues. An inscription at the palace of the Assyrian king Esarhaddon, from the seventh century BC, explains what was expected of these winged guardians:

Bulls and lions carved in stone,
which with their majestic appearance
deter wicked enemies from approaching.
The guardians of the stairway,
the saviours of the pathway of the king,
right and left, I placed them at the gates.

But not even the mighty power of these wise creatures can stand against the tides of time. Millennia of invasions and occupations, empires rising and falling and cultures ebbing and flowing have swept away the world they defended. The glory of Mesopotamia is long gone to ruins and dust, and the statues that once bound them to their duty are scattered among the museums of the world, their power lost. But, although the shedu no longer guard the palaces of Assyrian kings, and the lamassu no longer threaten thieves and assassins, the creatures themselves live on in their own magical realm. It's not entirely impossible that someone with the right knowledge could unlock the gates between worlds and call them back....

Pegasus
Majestic winged horse

Travelers in the mountains of Greece and Turkey—and perhaps as far north as the Caucasus range—might, if they're lucky or patient enough, catch a glimpse of a white shape flashing through the sky. Definitely not a plane, far larger than a bird, but as agile as any hawk, it wheels and turns in the clouds. If the fortunate mountaineer can follow it, and if the bright blur comes near enough to the rocks to be seen properly, an astounding form will be revealed. The huge and powerful body is that of a horse, but stronger and more graceful than even the finest thoroughbred, and a vast pair of eagle wings extend from just behind the shoulders. This is a *pegasus*.

Historically, Pegasus was the name of one particular creature. But that stallion's deeds were so legendary that its name was given to the entire race. Pegasus was the mount of Perseus, the great Greek hero who slew the Gorgon known as Medusa. Long after Perseus died—the pegasi can live for hundreds of years—Pegasus was again part of a famous monster hunt. When another hero, Bellerophon, was sent to destroy a *chimera* (see p. 116) that was ravaging the region of Corinth, the goddess Athena gave him a magic bridle with which he could tame and ride Pegasus. The hunt was successful, but Bellerophon arrogantly decided to keep Pegasus for himself and use the stallion to fly to Olympus, home of the gods. Zeus wasn't too happy about that; the god caused Pegasus to be stung by a horsefly, and the great winged stallion bucked the hero off to his death.

A pegasus, aside from the wings, at first glance conforms to the shape of extremely large thoroughbred horse, but there are a couple of key differences. First, the chest of a pegasus is much deeper and more solid than that of a mundane horse, to provide a solid anchor for the massive muscles that power its enormous wings. The immensity of its chest gives the graceful creature the appearance of being quite narrow in the abdomen. Second, the tail of the pegasus is almost twice as long, and far more muscular, than that of a terrestrial horse. In flight, this great tail acts as a rudder and drags on the ground when the pegasus is at rest.

Pegasi are quite intelligent, though completely wild and uncivilized, and generally despise and avoid contact with humans. It is impossible to capture and break a pegasus using normal means, although certain magical bridles can snare them. It is thought that the golden bridles worn by some of the *each uisge*, or *kelpies* (see p. 140) of the British Isles can work for this purpose. But the frightening prospect of fighting and defeating a kelpie, and then finding and breaking a pegasus, has kept this idea firmly theoretical.

Erinyes

Hideous agents of justice

They are dark as death and howl with vengeful rage, screaming out of the sky on bat wings of blackened brass. A tangled mane of hissing serpents, dripping venom, writhe around a face that's a hideous mingling of beautiful woman and blunt-muzzled dog. Eyes like slowly burning coal ooze thick tears of blood, the hot breath blowing a graveyard stench. Wrapped in dark, dirty robes of tattered rags, the right hand carries a smoking torch, the left a many-tailed scourge. It's an ancient irony that these horrible monstrosities—the *erinyes*—are responsible for punishing those who have sinned against nature.

The erinyes (the name is Greek) were known to the Romans as the Dirae, or Furies. In both Greece and Rome, they were so greatly feared that they were usually referred to, if they had to be mentioned at all, by one of many euphemistic names, such as *Semnai*, "the venerable," or *Eumenides*, "the kindly ones." This fear, and respect, is justified. Once fixed upon their target—one guilty of breaking the natural order by killing a parent, assassinating a rightful monarch or committing incest, for example—they are unceasing in their persecution. Although they sometimes attack physically, it's more common for the erinyes to attack their victims psychically, eventually driving he person insane. Once the victim is dead, the Dirae continue to torment the guilty soul in the underworld. Erinyes work in threes, the most famous trio of ancient times being Megaera, Alecto and Tisiphone.

As terrifying and merciless as the erinyes might be, it should be noted that they are neither malicious nor evil. Rather, they are the very personification of righteousness and inevitable justice. They aren't mindless or heartless, either, but quite intelligent and deeply emotional; their bloody tears are shed for the injustice and evil of mankind's crimes. If anything, the erinyes should be pitied, because their form and function keep them forever separate from all other company—when Tisiphone fell in love with a human man, for example, she accidentally killed him when a snake from her head bit and poisoned him.

Escaping the relentless Furies is, in most cases, impossible. The only way out is through divine intervention, such as when Orestes, the son of King Agamemnon, killed his father's murderer—his mother, Clytemnestra. The erinyes set upon him, driving him mad, until the goddess Athena absolved him of guilt and called the vengeful horrors off.

Piasa

Winged hybrid of Illinois

In 1673, while traveling on the Mississippi River near present-day Alton, Illinois, renowned Jesuit missionary Father Jacques Marquette and his companion, Louis Joliet, were the first Europeans to see, high on a sheer cliff face, a Native depiction of the creature known as the *piasa*. In his journal, Marquette, whose precisely accurate descriptions of such mundane creatures as bison must have seemed equally fantastic, described the creature in minute detail:

> "While skirting some rocks which by their height and length inspired awe, we saw upon one of them two painted monsters which at first made us afraid, and upon which the boldest savages dare not long rest their eyes. They are as large as a calf, have horns on their heads like those of a deer, a horrible look, red eyes, a beard like a tiger's, a face somewhat like a man's, a body covered with scales, and a tail so long that it winds all around the body, passing above the head and going back between the legs, ending in a fish's tail. Green, red and black are the three colors composing the picture."

Marquette's Native guides filled the missionary in on two important facts about the cliff painting. Firstly, the image itself was already ancient when their ancestors arrived in the area and were rendered by a people that had long since disappeared or migrated. Secondly, the creature depicted was wholly real.

The piasa is a monster of both water and air, as easily able to drag a large canoe into the depths as to fly off with a full-grown bison in its talons. It can cause thunderstorms and summon lightning and fierce winds and can create whirlpools and floods. The piasa's thick, scaled hide cannot be penetrated by spears or arrows—or, one presumes, bullets—but weapons anointed with certain powerful, poisonous herbs can bring it down.

Not much else is known about the piasa; researchers speculate that it was likely extinct or near extinction, even as Marquette was shown its image on the cliff. Others claim it as a folkloric combination—or confusion—of the *thunderbird* (p. 186) and a water monster such as the *mishipizhiw* (p. 108). Still others compare it to such diverse Asian and European monsters as the *roc* (p. 174) and the *manticore* (p. 128). Whatever the piasa was or wasn't—or is or isn't—it remains a favorite legend and mascot of southwest Illinois.

Roc
The great eagle

> It was for all the world like an eagle, but one indeed of enormous size; so big in fact, that its wings covered an extent of thirty paces, and its quills were twelve paces long, and thick in proportion. And it is so strong that it will seize an elephant in its talons, and carry him high into the air, and drop him so that he is smashed to pieces.
>
> —Marco Polo

Massive wings blot out the sun, the thunder of their beating like a thousand bass drums. The raptor's beak is the size and shape of a capsized fishing trawler. The feet are big enough to grasp a semi-trailer and tipped with talons resembling backhoe buckets. The long tail seems to stream for miles in the great bird's wake. The piercing cry is louder than a rocket engine. Once you've encountered the giant, eagle-like *roc*, you will never forget the sight.

If there is a king of birds—setting aside the semi-divine *garuda* of India (p. 176)—it must be the roc. Stockier in proportion than a true eagle—it more resembles an osprey—the roc's size is almost beyond imagining; in estimating its wingspan at 30 paces, the Venetian explorer Polo was, for once, understating reality, unless he meant the bird's wings spanned 30 paces *each*. That something so huge can fly is a miracle of biological adaptation. All birds have so-called hollow bones that keep their skeletons light enough to be airworthy, and the roc's are even less dense than usual, making the huge animal deceptively light. The roc's pinions and underfeathers are specially ducted to "air-condition" the giant body and prevent the roc from overheating from the massive exertion of flight.

Elephants are the usual food claimed by rocs in legend, but they aren't the bird's most common prey. Cattle and other large livestock, thoughtfully rounded up by human ranchers, are much more convenient. Neither are elephants the most spectacular food: sailors and fishermen have reported rocs diving for whales in the same way an osprey dives for fish, flying off slow and heavy with a 50-foot sperm whale flapping helplessly in its talons. A meal like that might feed a roc and its nestling chicks for two days. The parent bird (male and female rocs share the duties) drops chunks of meat into a feeding hole in the roof of a fortress-sized, dome-shaped nest woven from whole trees.

Garuda

Demon-hunting bird of India

Of all the world's great birds, the fierce *garuda* is considered the most noble. The *roc* (p. 174), though intelligent, has an animal's preoccupations, and the *phoenix* and *thunderbird* (p. 180 and p. 186) are almost impersonal forces of nature, but the garuda are an active ethical force, moral creatures with a righteous rage against all things evil and corrupt. Relentless predators, they hunt down malicious monsters, especially demons such as the shape-shifting *rakshasa*, wherever they find them.

In bright contrast to the dark things it fights are the garuda's rainbow plumage and majestic crest—shimmering blues mingled with brilliant flames of copper and gold, flecked and dappled with ruby, silver and jade in endless combinations unique to each individual bird. Its body is generally owl-like and grows steadily over its centuries-long lifetime, its wingspan extending from roughly 20 feet to its full growth of more than 20 yards. The garuda's owly face is very expressive and bears a human quality that's made more eerie by its hand-like feet. The talons, which are unusually long, are quite flexible and dexterous; garuda occasionally use weapons (mostly spears and lances) and have the habit of pointing and gesturing with one foot as they speak.

The garuda has a one-track mind, its concern the hunting and killing of demons. It's not that they're obsessed or maniacal, it's simply that their loathing of evil and dedication to righteousness is so great that they can't imagine anything else being important. They are natural detectives, and, when they've tracked down a monstrous threat, they'll attack without hesitation. The huge birds are genius fighters, and a team of two or three garuda is more than a match for even the most powerful of rakshasa.

Unlike many benevolent animals, garuda aren't particularly secretive, nor do they necessarily mind the company of humans; conversation with humans is, in fact, one of their best sources for information about monsters' whereabouts. Once you have its attention, enlisting the help of a garuda isn't difficult; the swift-flying birds will gladly check out even the most trivial report of bad luck or crop failure in search of their next battle.

Peryton

Living weapon of lost Atlantis

Atlantis. Of all the vanished lands of legend, none has had as powerful a hold on the imagination as this doomed island continent. When the most advanced societies were just discovering the secrets of agriculture, the people of Atlantis were raising great towers and laying out gardens; when others were doing battle with weapons of bronze, Atlantis fought wars with technology so advanced, it was indistinguishable from magic. These wars eventually destroyed the lost continent, and, although millennia have passed, some Atlantean weapons still exist. Among these weapons are the *perytons*, indestructible living weapons created by advanced genetics and sorcery.

The peryton, resembling a cross between a stag and an eagle, stands fully 10 feet tall. Its forequarters are those of a deer with iron-hard hooves, sharpened antlers and a mouthful of fangs instead of a normal deer's blunt herbivore teeth. The rest of the peryton is all bird, with taloned feet and huge wings. The iridescent green plumage is impervious to harm, and the indestructible peryton is effectively immortal. The magical nature of these twisted creations is revealed by the eerie man-shaped shadows they cast.

The perytons were designed in desperation and madness for use as shock troops, aerial scouts and airborne assassins against specific targets, rather than as a mass military force. They are bloodthirsty and remorseless, their ancient genetic programming leaving them no desire or purpose but to kill. The Atlantean engineers who designed these horrors had some degree of foresight, however, and built into their experimenttwo failsafe measures. First, perytons were designed to be sterile. Second, after killing one human, a biochemical change triggered in the peryton's brain renders it completely docile and compels it to return to Atlantis. With Atlantis destroyed, deactivated perytons either wander aimlessly in the wilds or plunge into the sea to rest forever on the ocean floor with the ruins of the civilization that created them.

Few active, homicidal perytons remain on Earth, which is cause for worry; by this time—many thousands of years after their activation—there shouldn't be *any*. There is speculation that a few perytons, perhaps only three or four of the thousands unleashed by Atlantis in its final wars, are capable of reproducing. If that is the case, these living weapons of mass destruction can continue to plague humanity for thousands of years to come.

Phoenix

Immortal firebird

Many supernatural creatures have become such potent images in human culture that they seem to have more reality as symbols than as real creatures, the virtues and vices they supposedly exemplify overshadowing the blood-and-bone reality behind the myths. The two main culprits in this confusion are the art of heraldry, which assigns specific (if not always appropriate) meanings to such creatures as the unicorn and the dragon, and the many branches of mysticism, magic and alchemy. In these, the *phoenix* took on great power as a symbol of spiritual awakening and rebirth, of the transmutation of metals and of the death and resurrection of Christ. But, unlike the unicorn, whose virtue is greatly exaggerated in myth, the phoenix's nature fits perfectly with the symbolic roles it has been given.

The phoenix is a strikingly beautiful bird of great size. Although it is nowhere near as large as the truly gigantic *roc* (p. 174), it attains a 15- to 20-foot wingspan when full grown. In body shape, it is more like a large and wonderfully graceful crane or ibis than a bird of prey. Its shining, metallic plumage comprises all the colors of fire: deep reds, brass and gold, shimmering blues and greens. The tail is long and flowing, like that of a show rooster or bird of paradise, and on the phoenix's head is a high, bright crest that shimmers like a halo of flame.

It is the phoenix's life cycle, however, that gives it its symbolic cachet. A phoenix can't be said to ever really "die"—or be "born," for that matter—because every four years, it renews and regenerates itself in a furnace of its own making. The phoenix spends most of its fourth year carefully building a large, domed nest of rare woods and special aromatic plants, often searching the world to find the proper materials. Once the nest is built, the phoenix enters, seals the nest wall behind itself and begins to increase its body temperature. This heating eventually causes spontaneous combustion in the materials of the nest, and, in a brief but terrifically hot and bright blaze, phoenix and nest are utterly consumed. From the pile of ashes, mineral-rich and still warm, a single phoenix hatchling then emerges, to begin the four-year cycle once more.

The means of the phoenix's seemingly miraculous regeneration are unknown, but theories exist. One suggests that the searing heat of the pyre somehow quickly incubates a dormant egg in the phoenix's body; others propose various magical or spiritual approaches. None can explain why there is more than one phoenix; how the phoenix population increases or replenishes its numbers is one of the great mysteries of supernatural ornithology.

Feng-hwang

The inseparable "phoenix of China"

Once on the Phoenix Terrace
the phoenix walked
Now the birds are gone
the terrace empty,
and the river flowing on...

—Li Bai (699-762),
"Climbing Phoenix Terrace at Jinling"

Of all the supernatural birds venerated around the world as sky deities or symbols of eternal mystical truths, none is so exquisitely noble as the sparkling flying jewels, the Masters of the South, the Lords of Summer, the Emperors of All Birds—the incomparable, and incomparably rare, *feng-hwang* of China.

Each feng-hwang is actually two birds, an inseparable mated pair. *Feng*, the cock, represents in Chinese symbolism the male yang principle and the sun. *Hwang*, the hen, represents the female yin and the moon. Physically, the feng-hwang resemble unusually graceful pheasants the size of large herons, with long plumage in iridescent shades of blue, red, white, gold and shimmering black. As with most birds, the feng's plumage is somewhat more garish than the hwang's, with a peacock-like fan of tail feathers; however, to call the hwang "dull" by comparison is akin to saying a ruby is duller than an emerald—both are dazzling visions of avian beauty.

Sometimes called the "Chinese phoenix," the feng-hwang, unlike the phoenix, which dies in flames and is reborn as a new bird, are truly immortal and spend much of their eternal lives on planes of existence other than the physical. Along with the *k'i-lin* (p. 138), the *dragon* (p. 114) and the tortoise, the feng-hwang is one of the cardinal animals of Chinese mythology—representing the South and Summer. They only manifest themselves on Earth in times of great wisdom, beauty and prosperity—or, perhaps, when a great evil threatens.

As you might imagine, the feng-hwang sing beautifully, their song said to have inspired the strangely haunting notes of the Chinese musical scale. And, as producers of heavenly music, they also appreciate great musical beauty: it is said that to have a feng-hwang overhear and be pleased by your playing, singing or poetry recitation is to ensure you great blessings.

Griffon

Lion of the skies

They appear on the banners and crests of countless nations and noble houses, symbols of strength and speed, nobility and relentless purpose...plus, they look really cool. Outside of the realm of heraldry and symbolism, they are the swiftest of airborne hunters, gliding silently over foothills and steppes from their cliff-side nests, diving like lightning on their prey...and looking even *cooler*. These are the legendary *griffons*, the most amazing killing machines in the world's skies.

The griffon appears as a monstrous blend of two great natural predators, with the hindquarters of a lion and the chest, wings, razor-sharp front talons and ripping beak of an eagle. Its lean and powerful feline body stands about five feet high at the shoulder, where its vast wings are anchored. The feathered chest is deep, to accommodate the massive flight muscles that enable the griffon to fly. Although the description of the griffon as a hybrid of eagle and lion is largely accurate, these creatures exhibit great variety in coloration, plumage and skull and beak shape; some are more panther than lion, others more hawk than eagle.

It might come as a disappointment to some, but the popular image of a griffon flying off with a horse in its talons isinaccurate. Flying is a strenuous business, and, though griffons do indeed crave horseflesh—a large griffon could conceivably lift one whole—the energy required to actually carry it away would be prohibitive. A griffon will gladly flap off with a medium-sized deer, but larger prey are either eaten on the ground or torn into manageable chunks for transport to cubs waiting in the nest. A favorite tactic with lighter prey is to swoop down, snatch it up and then drop it onto rocks from a great height, splattering an instant buffet dinner across the boulders.

Griffon nests are rumored to contain vast amounts of treasure, and this can sometimes be the case; like some birds, griffons love to collect and hoard shiny objects. But more often than not, after staking out horses as a decoy, climbing hundreds of feet up to the nest and braving the disemboweling talons and decapitating beaks of the aggressively defensive griffons, fortune hunters are greeted with a "treasure" of broken mirrors, chrome auto bumpers and pieces of colorful billboards. Better, and safer, odds are to stay home and play the lotto.

Monster Fact

Human livestock operations have allowed griffon populations to expand greatly from their home range on the Ukrainian/Russian steppes, but that area is still the only home of a rare, wingless subspecies of griffon known as the lesser, or "Scythian," griffon.

Thunderbird

Rider of the storm

Its habitat is the upper reaches of the sky, its gossamer-thin wings spanning hundreds of yards. The heart of the storm is its playground and dining hall, thunder and lightning its food and toys. It's revered as a god, and, from birth to death, its feet never touch the ground: the *thunderbird*.

Of all the world's monstrous avian species, the biology of the vast thunderbird is the most exotic, adapted as it has to a life lived entirely at high altitude. Its fully grown, translucent, albatross-like body is only about the size of a city bus, but the span of its delicate, membranous wings can stretch up to 550 yards. On these wings, the thunderbird soars constantly on the wind currents of the upper atmosphere. These strange birds don't even descend to Earth to lay their eggs; the tiny eggs are incubated in the insulation of the bird's plumage, and the chicks are able to glide from the moment they hatch.

Thunderbirds feed, breed and play in thunderstorms, diving down into the storm. Their broad wings serving as energy collectors, they feed on the electrical energy and lightning. Early spring is mating season, and violent spring storms swarm with thunderbirds caught up in the rituals of courtship. The males fight violently for mating rights, often to the death. The body of a thunderbird never reaches the ground, however; if its electrical field is disrupted, a dead thunderbird quickly disintegrates into water and fine ash.

Thunderbirds are not aggressive toward other creatures and have no natural enemies—not much else lives at the altitudes in which they thrive. They will defend themselves if provoked, however, lashing out with discharges of lightning from their supercharged internal batteries.

This lightning can prove dangerous to improperly shielded aircraft; an estimated 20 percent of airborne lightning strikes are defensive attacks from startled thunderbirds.

Will-o'-wisp

Treacherous light in the darkness

You don't generally plan on finding yourself lost in the middle of a stinking marsh on a moonless night, with the fog rolling in and the calls of night birds and unseen animals filling the damp air, but it happens. And when the sucking muck of the bog is dragging at your boots, the moss-hung trees are black-on-black shadows looming around you and each blind step is a potential step into a sinkhole, any light in the darkness is blessedly welcoming. This situation is what the elusive *will-o'-wisp* counts on.

If the will-o'-wisp has a physical form, it remains unknown; the thing appears as a variable floating light, changing from brightly glowing sphere to feeble flickering flame. Its color is blue, purple, pale green and, very rarely, white or yellow, and it meanders over the surface of the swamp, approaching then darting away, hovering low then popping up high, drawing the lost and bewildered wanderer along with it.

The will-o'-wisp isn't harmful in itself; it is the destination to which it leads its victims that does the harm. Those who follow the thing's flitting glimmer eventually find themselves on lethal ground—a sucking mud pit, a treacherous sinkhole, inescapable quicksand. *Why* it does this isn't clear; some speculate that will-o'-wisps are cruel night-flying faeries playing lethal pranks; others suggest that these ghostly lights are gaseous beings that feed off the swampy decomposition of their victims' bodies.

The unknown nature of these ephemeral beings makes it difficult to recommend a defense against them. If they are, in fact, faerie in nature, the usual measures against little folk—holy symbols, objects of iron, turning one's clothing inside-out and backward—might help. The wisest course, however, is to simply refuse to follow, but, given the almost hypnotic beckoning of these lights in the darkness, that's easier said than done.

Poltergeist

Baku

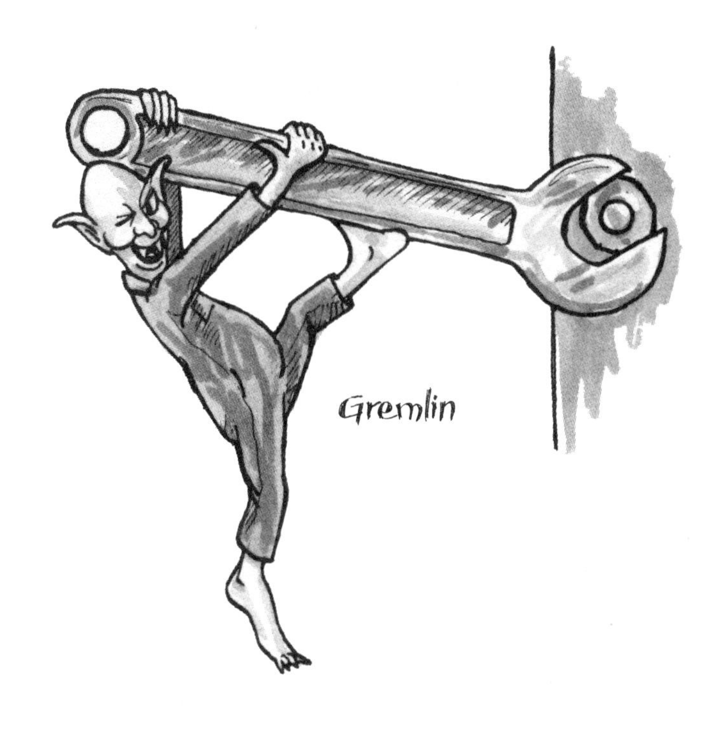

Chapter 6:

Mind over Matter

It´s a sound nobody wants to hear, a sound that once heard is never forgotten. It comes in the night, and when you hear that sound, that cry of mourning, like a woman having her soul torn out, all hope dies.

Tulpa

Mystic Tibetan thought-form

They call it the Roof of the World. At an average of more than 16,000 feet above sea level, the Tibetan Plateau seems to rise above the rest of the Earth, an enchanted land floating between heaven and the mud. Its thin air is haunted by strange magic, and powerful mystics wander its rugged mountains. These lamas (holy men) are known to have many incredible abilities, such as telepathy and the very handy power to be in two places at once. They are also the keepers of older, darker secrets of Tibet's hidden valleys. Of these strange talents, the one that concerns us is the ability of some mystics to create an independent creature of pure thought: a *tulpa*.

Through intense meditation and special rituals, the lama uses the powers of willpower and imagination to conjure up a perfect mental image of the being he or she wishes to create and then projects that image into the physical world. The tulpa can take any form, and as the mystic spends time and energy reinforcing its reality, it gradually becomes more tangible. Eventually, the tulpa becomes indistinguishable from a real person, with an ability to act independently, without direct control by its creator. This, as you might guess, is where the problems begin.

In her book, *With Mystics and Magicians in Tibet* (1931), explorer and Buddhist pilgrim Alexandra David-Neel describes her own experience with the tulpa. Over a period of several months of intense meditation, she succeeded in creating her own thought-being, "a monk, short and fat, of an innocent type." This jolly image, she writes, "grew gradually fixed and life-like looking. He became a kind of guest, living in my apartment." The monk joined her traveling party, performing "various actions of the kind that are natural to travelers and that I had not commanded."

Then the little monk started to go bad. "The features which I had imagined...gradually underwent a change. The fat, chubby-cheeked fellow grew leaner, his face assumed a vaguely mocking, sly, malignant look. He became more troublesome and bold. In brief, he escaped my control." Alarmed, David-Neel decided to dissolve the tulpa and only succeeded, she reports, "after six months of hard struggle. My mind-creature was tenacious of life."

She was right to end her experiment when she did—it's not unheard of for a powerful tulpa to kill its creator in the course of that final battle. An out-of-control tulpa can be surprisingly dangerous. Some wander off when sent out on a mission, becoming dangerously confused and illogical. Some, having no soul or conscience, become outright evil, almost demonic. Although most tulpa waste away when their creator eventually dies—which can take decades—some have the strength to keep themselves together. Walking the Earth might be dozens of these renegade thought-creatures, immortal, immoral and dangerously imperfect.

Baku

Japanese dream-eater

It's a natural law that wherever energy and opportunity exist, life will find a way to take advantage of it. Even at the bottom of the sea, where sunlight never reaches and the pressure can crush metal, living creatures cluster around thermal vents that expel heat and minerals from the Earth's core. This natural law is a supernatural law, too, and a good example of the law in action is the *baku* of Japan, a creature that consumes something humans generate in abundance: bad dreams.

The baku are creatures of the dream world and have no physical presence in the "real" world. As such, their appearance can vary as wildly as a dreaming person's imagination can make it. Generally, however, a baku is described as having a stocky but powerful body, like a cross between a lion and a tapir, covered in tawny fur, with either hooves or heavy, clawed paws. The head is elephant-like, with large floppy ears and a snout, shorter than an elephant's but still pronounced, with which it sucks up nightmares.

But bad dreams don't fade easily, and, though the baku has a sleepy, genial appearance, it is a fierce fighter. Normally, a dreamer will not even notice the presence of a baku; the only effect is having the nightmare replaced by a normal dream. But some bad dreams are so deeply rooted in the dreamer's mind that the baku can seem to be attacking the dreamer herself. In this case, the dreamer must defeat the baku in combat. The nearly immortal baku, however, just pretends to be defeated—the empowering feeling of victory releases the nightmare's grip on the dreamer, allowing the baku to safely feed.

Everything that eats produces waste, and the baku is no exception. After digesting the nightmares it consumes and, in the process, absorbing a lot of raw psychic energy, these mysterious dream creatures exude a universal form of positive energy. In other words, the baku excretes good luck! Many Japanese parents give their children baku dolls or figurines in the hope that they will attract these benevolent creatures to their home.

Poltergeist
The noisy ghost

> I don't care to deny poltergeists, because I suspect that later, when we're more enlightened, or when we widen the range of credulities, or take on more of that increase of ignorance that is called knowledge, poltergeists may become assimilable. Then they'll be as reasonable as trees.
>
> —Charles Fort,
> *The Book of the Damned* (1919)

It starts small: household objects going missing, new light bulbs burning out for no reason, breakables tumbling off shelves, bumps in the night. The cause? Earthquakes, maybe, or electrical faults. Maybe it's trucks or trains rumbling by. But the problems escalate. Stones fly out of nowhere to rain on unsuspecting victims, heavy furniture is dragged and toppled, unexplained fires flare up in empty rooms, sleep becomes impossible. Soon, the household becomes dangerous, unlivable, filled with the malevolent and destructive energy of the *poltergeist*.

For centuries it was believed that the poltergeist—German for "noisy spirit"—was a ghost or devil, a spirit creature that, for some reason, haunted a particular family and plagued them with mischief bordering on assault. Modern psychical research, however, has come up with a different theory. Noting the strong correlation between the presence of adolescent children—especially young girls—and poltergeist-type events, most researchers now hold that the phenomenon called "poltergeist" is, in fact, a psychic effect. The emotional turmoil of adolescence within the mind of a psychically gifted child, the theory goes, creates an unconscious manifestation of psychic power, especially when traumatic factors, such as a death in the family, a remarriage or abuse, are involved. The fact that a poltergeist will follow a family, rather than remain in one location, is held up as evidence for this hypothesis.

Neither the "ghost" nor the "psychic" explanation is entirely correct, however; the truth is much more complex and lies somewhere between the two. The poltergeist is, in fact, an independent entity but is neither ghost nor devil. It is a stable field of psychic energy, conscious but barely intelligent, that feeds off strong emotions. An invisible and immaterial mental parasite, it latches onto a receptive host and basks in her pain and anger. A side-effect of this contact is the creation of a powerful psychic field that begins to have an effect on the physical world. As the "haunting" continues, the fear and confusion it engenders makes matters worse and creates a vicious cycle.

Poltergeist activity is often mistaken for demonic possession. Poltergeist infestation and possession are in fact quite similar, though the former has no religious or spiritual aspect. The fact that exorcism is sometimes effective in eliminating a poltergeist is attributable to the same placebo effect found in the field of medicine: belief in the ritual causes the mind of the host to align itself in such a way that the parasite loses its grip on the psyche.

Gremlin

Spirit of mischief

Aboard an Allied bomber, high over wartime Germany, a freshly oiled and inspected bomb bay door jams tight for reasons unknown; later, it functions perfectly. In a modern oil refinery, engineers struggle for hours without success to find the source of a mysterious pressure drop somewhere in their miles of pipes and tubing, only to have the problem spontaneously resolve itself. In your own home, the keys that were "right there a second ago" vanish, only to reappear right where they belong after half an hour of searching. These events might be random glitches and frustrations...or they might be the work of the monkey-wrenching *gremlin*.

Known by many names and given many attributes around the world and throughout history, "gremlin" is a good generic name for these mischievous minor spirits. Although they seem to share the prank-pulling behavior of some faeries, and faeries are often blamed for gremlin actions, gremlins are an entirely different class of creature. Only semi-intelligent, they are invisible, immaterial and motivated by an elemental trickster humor—in effect, a gremlin is an autonomous bad-luck field.

Gremlin pranks are usually minor—relocating objects, causing small electrical failures and short-circuits, jamming light machinery—but they can have serious consequences if they're pulled at the wrong time. As primitive spirits, gremlins have a tendency to congregate in psychically "comfortable" places; if the psychic conditions are right, a nest of gremlins can haunt a certain person or place for long periods of time. The results are easily interpreted as the effect of some type of curse.

Because of their primitive, elemental nature, it's fairly easy to get rid of gremlins. Having little will or intelligence, they can be warded off by even the most basic charms—lucky rabbits' feet, dream catchers, statuettes of saints and other such mildly magical trinkets. Verbal spells and exorcisms work well, too, to the point where simply asking the gremlin politely to leave you alone will see the spirit on its way.

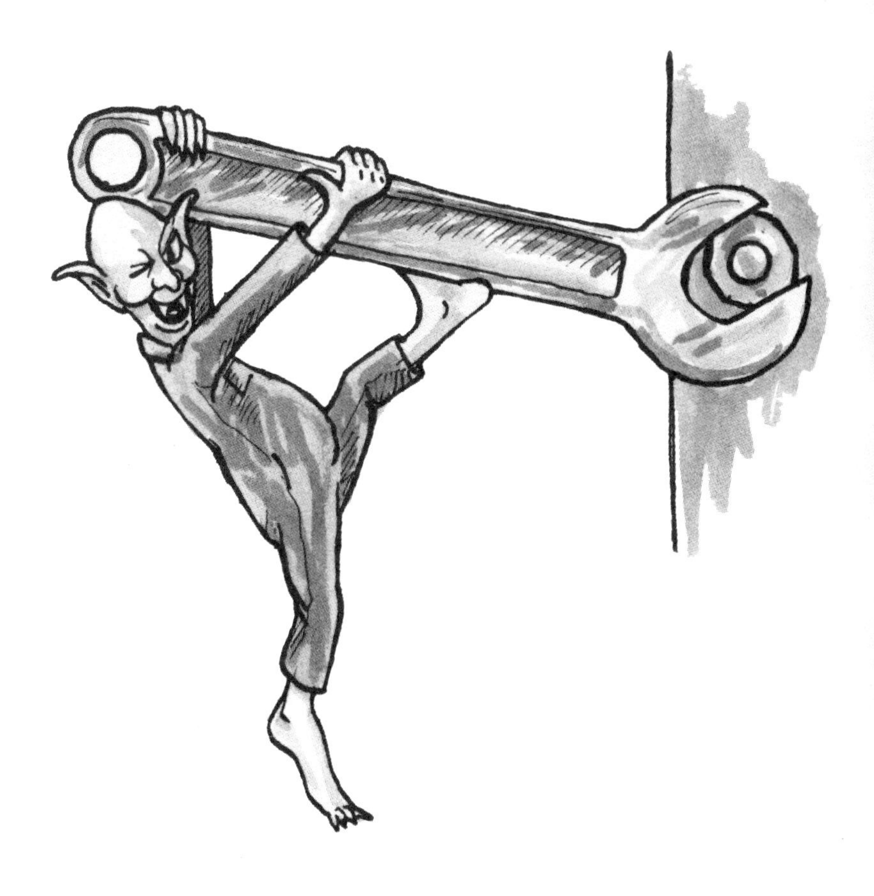

Incubus and Succubus

The sex demons

Life, whether natural or supernatural, is at its heart a system of energy exchange. So it is with one of nature's great founts of free energy, the human libido. Our wild sexual energy provides nourishment for the strange, seductive psychic vampires known as the *incubus* and *succubus*.

As energy beings, or spirits, these so-called "sex demons" have no physical form and rarely assume one, preferring instead to manifest themselves directly into the minds of their victims (if you can call them that), usually through dreams or dream-like states. The male incubi and female succubi appear as perfectly attractive specimens of their target's preferred gender; as the victim wishes, so will the vampire appear, generating maximum passion and arousal.

It's this passion on which the creature feeds, returning night after night to the same host, to bask in its glow. The dreams or waking visions of the victim, or host, are filled with sexual ecstasy, from the deepest forbidden desires to the purest joys of love. When he or she is awake, the psychic parasite's host often has little or no recollection of the night's events. Because the spirit only feeds off the excess energy generated by its own actions, there are few harmful side-effects, other than those associated with a lack of restful sleep.

The incubi and succubi tend to become quite attached to a single host. Unless induced to leave, they only move on when that host either becomes too exhausted to be a worth-while meal or develops the natural psychic defenses that make it too difficult for the creature to feed. Exorcism, prayer, meditation or sleeping pills easily drive a succubus away—and because their food is plentiful and readily available, there's no need for them so stay where they're not wanted.

Hag

The terrifying night witch

It's happened to almost everybody: you wake up after a long night of strange dreams and nightmares, sweating and hollow-eyed, disturbed and unfocused and feeling more tired than when you went to sleep. The symptoms might even occur over a series of nights, shortening your temper, ruining your concentration, sapping your energy. Stress, too much to eat before bed, too much coffee, the onset of a cold or flu—these are the mundane explanations. But these restless, draining nights can also be evidence of a visit from one of the inhabitants of the nightmare world, the sinister *hag*.

Although we've come to use the word "hag" to mean a grizzled and mean-spirited old woman, the hags that come in the night are not mortal beings. They might once have been evil human witches, but they now exist almost exclusively in the realm of dreams, in which they continue along the dark paths they followed in life. When they are perceived by their victims, which is rare, the impression they often give is of a wild and withered female of grotesque appearance, windblown and howling with malicious laughter, eyes burning, wrapped in tatters of unhealthy black. As a being of nightmare and dream, a hag can alter this impression at will.

Unlike other dream stealers, such as the *succubi* (p. 200), hags don't directly drain energy from their targets. Rather, they use their sleeping victims as a means to save energy, by having them serve as mounts, on which they ride through the nightmare world. On the dreaming backs of the sleepers, the hags ride through impossible worlds of darkness and fear, gleefully whipping and spurring their human mounts to greater and more terrifying speeds. The hag-ridden dreamer wakes clammy and exhausted, with no clear memory of what he or she has been subjected to during the night.

Any number of standard charms will ward away night hags. Like most vampires, psychic or physical, hags seek out the easiest targets. Those already prone to disturbed and unwholesome sleep are prime candidates for a hag ride. The best defense against the night witches is going to bed with a clear mind and a clean bloodstream.

Monster Fact

In addition to whatever enemies they make through their mysterious black magic, hags, like all evil dream creatures, have one great foe: the nightmare-eating *baku* (p. 194).

Banshee

The voice of mourning

It's a sound nobody wants to hear, a sound that once heard is never forgotten. It comes in the night, to those who've gathered around the bedside of a dying loved one. Even in those final hours, people carry their faint hopes; miracles happen, right? But when you hear that sound, that cry of mourning, like a woman having her soul torn out—the cry of the *banshee*—all hope dies.

The banshee is a female spirit (the Celtic root of her name, *ban sidhe*, means exactly that), and her role is to announce impending death, eternally pouring out her grief, along with mortal mourners. The banshee's wail is terrifying, but its message is seldom a surprise; the banshee is far more often heard at sickbeds than prior to unforeseen death. Hearing that heart-wrenching midnight cry, when none of your near and dear are known to be ill, is an especially powerful omen of doom.

A banshee's cry has a profound effect on those who hear it, even beyond its prophetic significance. It's simply one of the most horrible noises imaginable, an utterly hopeless sound that combines all the worst aspects of a sob, a scream and a moan. It extends beyond the range of human hearing, into the realm of high-frequency ultrasound and low-frequency infrasound. Sound waves in these ranges have marked physical effects on humans. Even if you're "not afraid of ghosts," the banshee's cry will induce uneasiness, despair, nausea and possibly temporary partial paralysis.

The banshee is generally regarded as the ghost of some long-dead woman with a tragic story—a scorned lover who drowned herself, a mother who lost her children to fever or plague or something equally poetic. Such is almost never the case. Banshees are independent spirits, and, although some research suggests that they are psychically or mystically drawn to places marked by tragic death, they are not ghosts.

Monster Fact

Military researchers are interested in using the same sound frequencies as those found in the bloodcurdling cry of the banshee as "sonic weapons." These weapons project high- and low-frequency tones beyond the range of human hearing to immobilize or demoralize enemies without lethal force.

Monsters I Have Found:

Notes: ______________________________

____

____

____

Notes: ______________________________

____

____

____

Author's Bio

Darren Zenko

Darren Zenko is a freelance journalist, alternative-radio broadcaster, pop-culture commentator and karaoke host.

Darren's lifelong fascination with the paranormal began as soon as he read Reader's Digest's *Strange Stories, Amazing Facts*. It continued with an attempt to summon the ghost of Elvis in his junior high industrial-arts darkroom and ultimately led him to pursue a writing career in the area. Darren is the author of several best-selling ghost story books, including *Ghost Stories of Pets and Animals* and *Werewolves and Shapeshifters*.